Terrorist Attack

Rooted to the ground, the FBI agents watched the van jump the curb. It heaved onto the sidewalk, jounced for a moment, then roared across the plaza. On a collision course with the Federal Building's glassed lobby.

The shock wave blew the agents through a dry cleaner's storefront window. That saved their lives.

The Federal Building's facade rippled upward, forty-seven stories of glass transformed to mist. The debris climbed into the air above the building like a reaching hand.

But then gravity took hold. An avalanche of rubble—glass, concrete, splintered wood, wiring, the remains of furniture, of bodies—thundered into the street with the force of a pyroclastic flow.

THE SIEGE

NOVELIZATION BY
Lewis Gannett

STORY BY
Lawrence Wright

SCREENPLAY BY
Lawrence Wright
and
Menno Meyjes & Edward Zwick

DIRECTED BY
Edward Zwick

HarperEntertainment
A Division of HarperCollinsPublishers

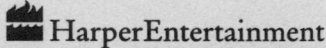
HarperEntertainment
A Division of HarperCollins*Publishers*
10 East 53rd Street, New York, N.Y. 10022-5299

Thanks to Myles Aronwitz, Bill Foley, and Merie W. Wallace
for the interior photographs.

This is a work of fiction. The characters, incidents, and
dialogues are products of the author's imagination and are not to be
construed as real. Any resemblance to actual events or persons,
living or dead, is entirely coincidental.

ISBN 0-06-102004-4

HarperCollins®, ☰®, and HarperEntertainment® are trademarks of
HarperCollins*Publishers* Inc.

Cover photo copyright © 1998 and courtesy of
Twentieth Century Fox Film Corporation.

First printing: December 1998

Printed in the United States of America

Visit HarperEntertainment on the World Wide Web at
http://www.harpercollins.com

❖ 10 9 8 7 6 5 4 3 2 1

THE SIEGE

PROLOGUE

At 12:32 P.M. Eastern Standard Time, CNN interrupted its regular programming with a "Breaking News" report that would horrify much of the world.

Much of the world. Not all of it. CNN's story involved the ongoing confrontation between the United States and Saddam Hussein. A massive explosion had ripped through a U.S. military barracks on the outskirts of Dhahran, Saudi Arabia. The barracks housed troops responsible for keeping a lid on the no-fly zone in southern Iraq. Although details were sketchy—the explosion had occurred only twenty-six minutes before—a handful of facts had been established. Several hundred servicemen called the building their home away from home. Because the explosion hit at 10:00 P.M., Dhahran time, most of the men were presumed to have been in their quarters, likely asleep in bed.

Officials conceded the probability of a major loss of life. They also confirmed that a terrorist action was the suspected cause. Beyond that, grim-faced Pentagon and White House spokespersons had little to say, citing a scarcity of information and "national security concerns."

The story hijacked the day's news cycle and didn't let go. By 1:00 every American television network, and many foreign networks, had suspended regular programming to cover the crisis. CNN carried the first live television images at 1:11, courtesy of SSTC, Saudi State Telecommunications Corporation. Under klieg lights and a pale moon in the cloudless desert sky, the scene conveyed the singularly destructive power of modern plastic explosives.

Eight stories of cinder blocks and reinforced steel, the barracks had been sturdily built. But the explosion sheared off the facade—literally blew it away—exposing the warren of rooms within. Not much remained of the interior. Walls, floors, and doors appeared to have been subjected to a giant blowtorch. The remnants of furniture and fixtures clogged the exposed floors, dangled from them, indeed fell from them, a slow-moving cascade of debris as walls and beams gave way. Flames blazed in the upper stories, seemingly impervious to water jetting from military fire trucks. Around the gutted structure dozens of emergency lights flashed from ambulances and official vehicles, strobing a frantic rescue effort by medics and soldiers as they probed mountains of rubble in search of life. Astoundingly, given the force of the blast, hundreds of men had in fact survived. But many met grimmer fates. The video images zeroed in on multiple variations of a grisly, too-familiar sight— medics zipping mangled corpses into body bags.

By 2:20 that afternoon ABC and CBS were pooling a live satellite feed from the British Broadcasting Corporation. A BBC news team had just wrapped up a week-long documentary shoot on the state of military readiness in the region, only to discover that their story possessed unexpected new dimensions. American channel surfers migrated in droves to ABC and CBS. While Saudi Telecommunications was generating vivid video, its reporters lacked the English-language fluency that Derek Thorngold, the BBC correspondent, was only too glad to put to use.

Thorngold described a pandemonium of confusion, shock, and mass death. He also noted the professionalism of the soldiers and medics who were attempting to save lives. Riveted, millions of Americans watched and listened; millions more listened by radio in cars and offices across the land. The essentials Thorngold laid out called to mind other murderous catastrophes that had rocked the U.S. in recent years. The bombing of New York City's

World Trade Center. The bombing of Oklahoma City's Federal Building. The devastating attacks on the Marine Corps barracks and embassy in Lebanon. Truck bombs had been used in all four cases. In three of them, Arab terrorists executed the bombings; Americans, of course, were responsible for the Oklahoma blast. Here in Dhahran, Thorngold went on, a truck bomb was also implicated. An unmarked medium-size utility truck, of a make used for general-purpose deliveries all over the Middle East, had somehow been permitted to approach the barracks. The driver jumped out and fled in a waiting Mercedes. Minutes later, before the barracks' security forces could respond, the truck exploded.

The perpetrators almost certainly were Arab terrorists, Thorngold continued. Their motivations? While it was much too early to say with certainty, the most likely explanation concerned one aspect or another of the U.S.'s stranglehold on Iraq. The aftermath of the Gulf War against that nation, and the ensuing conflict over the issue of weapons inspections had brought a substantial American military presence to countries that either bordered Iraq or were situated nearby—most notably Kuwait, but Saudi Arabia and a number of the smaller Gulf states as well. Not everyone was pleased with this arrangement. In Saudi Arabia public opinion was sharply divided. Could this most recent bombing be a local protest? Entirely possible, Thorngold declared. Though well policed—in fact, brutally policed—Saudi Arabia harbored a shadowy resistance movement. On the other hand, the bombing could be the work of any number of disaffected groups in the region. Conceivably, it could be the work of Saddam himself.

Bottom line, Thorngold concluded, finding the perpetrators would require a lengthy and tedious investigative process. A patience-trying process. It would be nice to avenge the deaths with terrible swift force. And, of course, perhaps most important of all, it would be nice to feel as if the West could defend itself from cowardly attacks.

But the real world of the Middle East was not a nice place, Thorngold warned. The grieving families and fellow citizens of the slain soldiers would have to wait for retribution.

Americans once again were forced to face a disturbing paradox. Their country possessed the most formidable fighting machine in the history of the human race. But what use was such power against enemies who could come from nowhere, inflict great harm, and then vanish—invisibly, anonymously—into the night? Was there any assurance that American law enforcement could find the terrorists? Any assurance that it could even identify them?

Later in the day, at a televised White House

press conference, President Clinton told the nation that no effort would be spared. He vowed that the appropriate American authorities would "go to any lengths, anywhere in the world, to bring these people to justice."

But as months, then years, went by, the terrorist mastermind behind the attack remained anonymous. And at large.

Unexpectedly, that situation would change.

1

TYRE, LEBANON

The four-door Mercedes sedan roared down the ancient road, leaving a luminous wake of sand and dust. Ocean sparkled to one side, the azure waters of the eastern Mediterranean. Scrub barrens stretched away on the other side, brownly arid, a near desert. Occasional date palms fringed the shoreline, their crowns frowsy but jaunty against the white-hot sky.

Caravans of forgotten civilizations had passed ancestors of these trees, traveling the main land route between what would become Europe and what would become the Middle East. Indeed, bands large and small had swarmed along this coast for thousands of years, straight through to the modern era, seeking fortune, salvation, all manner of destiny. Multiple dangers complicated their quests: armed brigands, holy warriors, heat, more heat, the age-old scarcity of fresh water. Who could say how many adventurers had perished here below the palms, beneath the pitiless sun?

No one could say. Sand, wind, and dryness had long ruled the coast of what is now called Lebanon, ravening forces of nature that quickly reduced death to dust. Uncounted human remains had disappeared along the wayside, leaving no trace of their grief.

But the modern era had brought some exceptions. The Mercedes hurtled past the burnt-out hulks of Russian T–54 tanks. Latter-day beasts of war, they lay askew and stripped beside the road, stubbornly resistant to the claim of the land.

In time, of course, they too would erode to dust. The Mercedes' swarthy occupants didn't give the tanks a glance. Two men sat up front, a third occupied the rear. The driver and the man beside him concentrated on the road, their deadpan demeanors and solid physiques hinting at a line of work that featured guns—a commitment to put themselves, if need be, in harm's way. The man in back was older, verging on elderly. His turban, hennaed beard, expensive sunglasses, and sere air marked him as a person of status. People deferred to this man. They looked up to him. They feared and obeyed him.

Which wasn't to say that he himself had nothing to fear. This man had lived with threats for a very long time. Only his wiliness and the devotion of his followers had kept him alive into his sunset years. To him, vigilance was a way of life. Every moment of every day, he awaited attack. And for this he was well prepared.

But prepared though he was, neither he nor his guards could have imagined the adversary they soon would encounter.

A SECRET COMMAND POST, SOMEWHERE IN THE USA

A man wearing a perfectly tailored suit sat before an electronic workstation in a small, windowless room. High-definition digital monitors dominated the station, which otherwise was devoted to communication links—phones, radios, data terminals, electronic messaging screens. Apart from the hum of several mainframe computers lining the walls to the left and the right, and occasional beeps from the messaging screens, the room was quiet. A console at the far end held an interconnected array of small-scale computing devices that hadn't been styled to compete in the consumer marketplace. Complex but utilitarian, advanced but somehow improvised in appearance—almost as if jury-rigged—the machines performed specialized tasks. The kind of tasks that a military tactician, not a commercial number cruncher or a tech-obsessed geek, would have reason to fulfill.

The man sitting at the workstation, though not in uniform, was a military tactician. General William Devereaux of the United States Army had pulled off numerous special operations over the course of a distinguished career. In his late forties, he carried himself with ease, his body limber under the perfectly tailored suit. Clean-shaven, his hair close-cropped, his nose straight, discipline etched in the lines bracketing his mouth, he emitted the confidence—the control—of one who is accustomed to wielding power, putting it to precise use.

General Devereaux stared at the blank screen before him, a faint smile on his lips. In less than a minute he would attempt his most elegant coup to date.

The high-res monitor self-activated. On it a digital readout counted down: 50, 49, 48. . . . The general studied the countdown, his eyes icily focused, a distinct state of consciousness pervading his mind: 31, 30, 29. . . . A state of clarity: His thoughts were blades, slicing the thin air: 18, 17, 16. . . .

Devereaux leaned forward to a microphone. He waited until the countdown reached 11. As it hit 10, he said softly, "All units: ten seconds."

The digits progressed: 9, 8, 7, 6, 5, 4, 3, 2. . . .

Devereaux flipped a switch, accessing data streams he'd established without the knowledge of the National Security Agency technocrats whose systems he had diverted to highly irregular use. The countdown vanished.

A grainy spy-satellite image flashed on-screen.

It showed a narrow, winding road with water to one side, brownish terrain to the other. Readouts specified the geographical coordinates of the area under surveillance; status indicators glowed, telling the general that all elements were on track. Very slightly, his pulse quickened.

He declared into the microphone, "We're on-line for exactly two minutes."

A car, shimmery in the satellite's eye but identifiable as a Mercedes, sped down the road, trailing clouds of dust. Some distance away an aggregation of small shapes, a few dozen in all, drifted toward the road. Herd animals of some kind: sheep, or goats. The general's smile tightened. He was seeing what he wanted to see, needed to see, down to the last detail.

Two shepherds, dressed in the traditional *djellaba* robes of nomadic tribesmen, goaded a herd of sheep across the dry scrubland outside Tyre, Lebanon. In the background a cloud of dust crept into the air, behind a speeding Mercedes. The shepherds paid scant attention to the car. Like the wrecked tanks that littered the area, like the jet combat aircraft that periodically tore apart their skies, it represented a world far removed from their way of life. The sheep neared the road. The Mercedes, still a hundred yards away, was bearing down at over eighty miles an hour and showed no signs of slowing. But to the sheep and the shepherds, the car didn't really exist. Bleating gently, the herd surged onto the pavement.

The Mercedes' driver cursed. He mashed his horn, kept it mashed, and didn't slow.

More sheep crowded onto the road, oblivious to the oncoming mass of high-grade steel. One of the shepherds paused by the roadside. With weathered fingers he unbuttoned his fly. Sighing contentedly, he peed.

Again the driver cursed. This pitiful pair of shepherds could not know whom they were obstructing. When they found out they would be dismayed, and most certainly would regret inconveniencing his most eminent holiness, the Sheik Ahmed bin Talal. Jaws clenched, the driver kept the pedal to the metal.

Through the satellite-imaging system that didn't quite read license plates, but came close enough, General Devereaux watched the Mercedes zip toward the sheep. A collision appeared imminent. The general wasn't worried. He said almost languidly, "Slow down."

The Mercedes' driver couldn't hear the general. But as if on command, the tiny car slowed.

*   *   *

The shepherds ignored the car as it ground to a halt amid billowing wreaths of dust. The driver and the bodyguard glared at the sheep milling on the pavement, a barricade of dingy, mindless fleece. Then the driver noted the stream of urine hissing from the *djellaba* into the dry roadside soil. He lowered his window, stuck out his head, and commenced screaming in salt-laced Arabic.

The shepherd straightened, signaling at last his comprehension that the road served a purpose more important than accommodating his herd. Hurriedly, he rebuttoned his fly; modesty required him to turn from the car.

Or so thought the vexed driver, bodyguard, and sheik. In fact, modesty had nothing to do with the shepherd's posture. Metal glinted within his *djellaba's* commodious sleeve: the silenced muzzle of a Colt Commando CAR–15.

Bleating, aware in their dim way that trouble was brewing, the sheep ambled from the road. It took twelve seconds or so for them to clear the way. During that span of time their plodding hooves and gentle cries masked a succession of thuds.

Lethal thuds: Both shepherds turned, aimed, and unleashed fusillades of silenced automatic fire. The Mercedes' windshield evaporated into tiny shards. The driver convulsed, then slumped over the wheel. His front-seat companion heaved through the destroyed window, half-sprawling onto the hood. Blood sprayed, filming jagged glass with red. With stunning speed the Mercedes had been transformed into coastal Lebanon's most recent *abattoir*.

The shepherds weren't done. They pulled the shaking but unscathed sheik from the car and hustled him some distance down the road. Working in tandem, they rapidly prepped their victim—trussed him, as if dressing a giant bird—for the next stage of his misadventure.

One shepherd secured a black hood over the sheik's head. The other shepherd injected him with a hypodermic syringe. Then he extracted a canvas satchel from his robe, activated a switch, and swung the satchel into the Mercedes. Meanwhile, the first shepherd secured a lightweight carbon-filament harness around the sheik's chest. A cable connected the harness to a box on the ground; the box opened, releasing a balloon that self-inflated with industrial vigor. The balloon hurtled aloft, drawing taut the cable and plucking the sheik from the road. Up he went, ascending higher and higher into the white-hot sky.

Sheik Ahmed bin Talal was losing consciousness, a consequence of the injection he'd received. Moreover, the hood over his head deprived him of vision. But just before he blacked out he grasped a number of realities—images, sounds, phantasmic sensations—that would linger in his mind like the remnants of a very bad dream.

He imagined his car and his dead men dwindling below him as he continued to rise. He imagined the shepherds and the sheep and the road swiftly shrinking, acquiring the dimensions of toys. A loud banging noise echoed from the ground—an explosion of some kind. The destruction of evidence, of the car? And then, eeriest of all, the sheik heard the roar of an approaching aircraft.

It got louder, then ominously much more loud. The plane sounded as if it were flying right at him. No, the sheik realized, his thoughts fraying. Not at him—the plane was passing directly above. Targeting the balloon? Why? To kill him? *This execution featured a series of bizarre aerial stunts?*

Suddenly the cable jerked once again, but this time not in a vertical direction. *The plane has caught the cable,* the sheik thought with terror. And now was dragging him through a turbulent slipstream at hundreds of miles an hour. . . .

On the ground, the shepherds watched the MC–130 combat Talon aircraft head out to sea, the cable snagged in its nose cone "whiskers." The sheik, limp now, unconscious, probably grateful to be unconscious, dangled helplessly below.

When he revived he would find himself aboard a commercial ship leased to an obscure Cayman Islands commodities broker, under the command of tight-lipped American intelligence officers.

The satchel bomb that had blown up the Mercedes continued to burn, sending a column of black smoke into the air.

The sheep, bleating, took in the scene with indifferent eyes.

General Devereaux took in the scene with satisfied eyes. "Gotcha," he exclaimed softly as the plane moved off-screen.

The satellite image broke up in a blur of static.

Devereaux had been on-line for exactly two minutes. But he'd only needed two minutes to literally snatch from the face of the earth one of America's most dangerous enemies.

A SAFE HOUSE

Sheik Ahmed bin Talal, less self-possessed than he was accustomed to feeling, sat in his cell at a steel-case table. No decor adorned the cell, no luxuries softened its fixtures. In addition to the table and a couple of chairs, the sheik's surroundings consisted of a steel toilet, a steel cot, impregnable walls, and an impregnable steel door. Closed-circuit video cameras pointed from the ceiling's corners.

Across from the sheik sat General William Devereaux, cool and crisp in an immaculate suit. The general said dispassionately, "Nobody knows you're here." The sheik regarded him with hooded eyes. "Not even my president," Devereaux went on. The sheik, mute, absorbed those words. "You'll die here alone and be buried unknown. Barring some miracle."

The sheik mumbled a few words in Arabic.

"God?" Devereaux said, his eyes acquiring a quizzical glow. "*God?*" He stared at his prisoner. "What you eat. *Whether* you eat. Sleep. Pain. Absence of pain—*I* decide. I make the day and the night. Even the way you got here . . ." The general paused, giving the sheik a moment to consider the enormity of his predicament. "A hand that reached down from the sky?"

The sheik suppressed a shudder. He remembered only too well the snatching hand.

Devereaux sustained his stare. "God?" he asked once again. "I am your new God."

The sheik was a stern man, and a tough man. He'd dealt with many players in the Middle East's game of power chess. Ruthless players. Clever players. Players who gave no quarter.

Here, he might finally have met his match.

2

If the nature of the sheik's God was in dispute at the safe house, elsewhere the Muslim faith flourished unchallenged.

Dawn filtered into the cavernous mosque. A robed man climbed the minaret's spiral staircase, his slippered feet noiseless on stone steps. The *muezzin*, the crier who called believers to prayer five times a day, entered a turretlike room in the minaret's top and clicked on a microphone. *"Allahuh Akbar!"* he chanted in the sonorous rhythms of liturgical Arabic. His amplified voice echoed through the mosque and the streets without. As they had done for centuries, the faithful responded.

Dim under its high dome, its walls decorated with calligraphic and geometric motifs, the central prayer hall held hundreds of worshipers. They prostrated themselves in the same direction, toward the wall that held the *mihrab*, an arch that identified the wall as the mosque's closest to the holy city of Mecca. Hundreds of foreheads lowered to prayer carpets on the tiled floor. Twice as many hundreds of shoes huddled in pairs just inside the entrance, work boots, expensive loafers, sandals, sneakers, glossy dress brogues. While gender played a role in the organization of this place—women worshiped in a separate gallery—social rank counted for nothing. All classes, rich and poor, learned or not, were welcome.

The observances extended beyond the mosque. In the neighborhood outside, in shops and open-air bazaars, in homes decorated with traditional Arab artifacts, on sidewalks redolent of the sweet, thick coffee of the Middle East, people heard the *muezzin*'s echoing chants and knelt to pray.

Such scenes might lead one to conclude that the mosque stood on Islamic territory, its graceful spires pointing at a Muslim sky. For those heeding the day's first call to worship, that, of course, was the case. But spires of a different sort also greeted the dawn above this city, claiming a variety of spiritual and secular stakes. Across an expanse of water known as the East River rose a famous skyline—the towers of downtown Manhattan.

Brooklyn, New York, was home to this mosque and the thriving transplantation of Islam in the neighborhoods beyond.

*   *   *

Across the river, early risers went about their business in the World Trade Center, on Wall Street, in the canyons of the business capital of the world. The Federal Building, a forty-seven-story downtown tower that housed the offices of United States government agencies, was no exception.

Two FBI agents hurried through the bullpen in the situation room on the twenty-second floor. Tina Osu, thirty-two, of Japanese descent, combined sharp good looks with professional poise. Frank Haddad, two or three years older, Lebanese by birth and an American citizen since the age of eleven, had been with the FBI a solid decade. His grin could light up a room.

The two agents had encountered each other in the hall outside. Tina informed Frank tersely, "Brooklyn South issued a code blue less than two minutes ago. They think hostages are involved."

"Police on the scene?" Frank asked.

"Setting up a perimeter right now," Tina replied.

"Residence or business?"

"A bus," Tina said.

A bus, Frank thought. "Code blue" alerts designated situations in which a locale, usually a building, had been commandeered by means of armed force. *Why would someone devote such energy to a bus? In Brooklyn?*

Frank and Tina served on the Joint FBI/NYPD

Terrorism Task Force. The fact that the Task Force had been alerted to this problem suggested that the bus, whatever the motivations of the people who held it, could be in serious trouble indeed.

The Brooklyn street was cordoned off. In the center stood a #99 bus, its crosstown route brought to a halt. A phalanx of sky-blue NYPD cars surrounded the bus, providing a perimeter behind which cops crouched, guns drawn.

From hastily formed police lines, a mixture of local residents and early-morning commuters whose transit had been interrupted watched bemusedly. Curiosity more than fear motivated the spectators. What could hijackers hope to gain from this crime? They clearly were going nowhere. Not with this many cops on the scene.

Then the rumors started circulating. The hijackers had connected an ominous-looking canister to the bus's door. No one knew for sure if the canister contained a bomb. But the police seemed to think so; specially trained officers were evacuating the adjacent buildings. Then came even more disquieting news. The canister was also connected to the bus's windows; if the door or any of the windows were opened even a crack, the bomb would blow—supposedly. The passengers, it seemed, were trapped. Strangest of all, according to those in the know, the perpetrators had set up this bomb-on-wheels in a matter of minutes—then had left. Apparently they weren't on the bus after all. They'd wired it, told the passengers to stay put, and *disappeared*.

As sirens converged, and the crowd grew bigger, tension mounted. The bus could go up at any moment.

An imposing African-American man strode into the FBI situation room, joining Tina Osu and Frank Haddad. Age thirty-six, six feet two inches tall, one hundred and eighty pounds of muscle encased in a sober suit, he was Anthony Hubbard, known to friends and colleagues as Hub. One of four Assistant Special Agents in Charge at the FBI's twelve-hundred-agent Manhattan office, he led the Joint FBI/NYPD Terrorism Task Force. The #99 bus in Brooklyn accordingly fell in his jurisdiction. It was his baby.

"SWAT?" Hub demanded.

"On the way," Frank said.

"Negotiator?" Hub asked, concern furrowing his brow.

"Rolling," Tina affirmed.

"Bomb squad?" Hub said, his questions rapid-fire.

Frank and Tina nodded.

"Let's go," Hub declared to Frank. They headed for the door.

Tina stayed put. She would track the Task

Force's response from headquarters, providing interagency coordination if the crisis escalated.

The bomb-squad truck rolled through Brooklyn, siren wailing. Cops waved it past the police line; the truck halted behind the cordon of cop cars. Men dressed in what appeared to be space suits emerged. The bulky helmets and tough Mylar fabric could withstand fairly serious blasts. Not Semtex plastic explosive going up at close range, of course. But the suits did a nice job of fending off flames and flying glass.

In the bus, terrified passengers watched the bomb squad approach. The sight produced mixed feelings. On the one hand, experts had arrived, definitely a good thing. On the other hand, the experts' protective gear underscored what might happen to unprotected flesh; it made the possibility that the passengers could be ripped to shreds more real. A woman comforted her trembling daughter. A young Asian couple hugged. Two elderly men exchanged incredulous stares. None of them had ever expected to experience something like this. Not here, on the streets of Brooklyn, New York. In an ordinary, everyday #99 bus.

Hub and Frank Haddad exited the Federal Building's glass-fronted lobby and took in the beginnings of rush hour on Broadway.

Hub looked at Frank. "How soon can we get there?" he asked, already knowing the answer. Not fast enough.

"In this traffic," Frank replied with a shrug, "maybe tomorrow."

Hub didn't laugh. The two men strode across Federal Plaza, a paved expanse that separated the building from the street, toward the Bureau's garage. Hub considered taking the subway. The closest station happened to be City Hall / Brooklyn Bridge; a one-stop jump over the East River would put them in downtown Brooklyn. Unfortunately, however, the #99 bus hadn't been waylaid in downtown Brooklyn. And Brooklyn was a big place.

They would have to fight traffic in Hub's unmarked car.

The bomb squad made progress with the bus. A technician finished drilling a hole in its door. He extracted an instrument from his tool kit: a small dental mirror mounted on a seven-inch stem. Carefully, he inserted the mirror in the hole, to get views of the canister and the wiring that connected it to the door. The passengers watched with bated breath. The mirror rotated like a robot's precision-guided servomechanism. This technician seemed to know what he was doing.

But then the canister started to hiss.

The passengers recoiled with petrified gasps;

the hiss sounded businesslike, portentous, the precursor of something lethal. Screaming, they scrambled for cover, slamming themselves behind seats, diving to the aisle's floor.

An explosion rocked the bus. Wetness filled it—a spray of viscous liquid, thicker than water, and warm.

The bus's double doors blew outward. Like an invisible hand, the shock wave smacked the bomb squad from their positions. Behind the police lines, spectators screamed. Cops winced, cursed, and leapt to their feet, breaking cover to see what could be done. Not much, it appeared. As if spray-painted, the bus's interior had been coated with dark fluid. It didn't take a lot of imagination to guess the fluid's origin.

The car inched toward the access ramp to the Brooklyn Bridge. Frank's cell phone rang.

"Haddad," Frank told the phone. He listened a few seconds. Hub sent him an apprehensive glance. "Oh, fuck," Frank muttered, meeting Hub's eyes. "It just blew."

Hub took a deep breath; they should have resorted to the subway after all. His grip on the steering wheel tightened.

Officers approached the bus warily, in the trance that accompanies human reaction to an unspeakable event. Time slows down for those beholding the aftermath of such events, the result of not wanting to know what has happened, but nonetheless perceiving details with hyperclarity. For example, the bus's double doors hanging off their hinges; something disheveled about that, heart-rendingly sad. The fluid flowing from the doors, dribbling to the pavement, steaming thickly in the chill air. Coagulating already.

The lead cop noticed something that stopped him dead in his tracks. The fluid wasn't red. It was blue. Bright blue.

He saw movement in the bus. Then he heard whimpers, and muffled sobs. Somehow, people had remained alive in there.

Not only were they alive, they were getting to their feet, grabbing seats for balance, moving along unsteadily—stupefied, the cops watched passengers stumble to the door.

They emerged, tumbling down the steps, collapsing into outstretched arms—their dazed eyes taking in a world they'd thought they would never rejoin—and it became clear that the victims weren't covered with blood.

They were covered with blue paint.

Frank got the news over his cell phone and relayed it to Hub.

"*What?*" Hub exclaimed, his eyes flashing.

"That's what they're telling me," Frank replied. The denouement of the bus drama had an odd effect on Frank. Something about it made him want to laugh. In Hub's presence, under these circumstances, that wasn't a good idea.

"And nobody's hurt?" Hub asked with disbelief.

Frank nodded. Hub closed his eyes; who could have expected that a code blue situation would end in such a bizarre fashion, with a paint job in blue? He felt a surge of gratitude mingled with relief. Fighting terrorism for a living had taken a toll on him; in his experience terrorist actions rarely ended happily. "Thank God," he murmured.

Still, something about the incident disquieted Hub. He had a hunch that it hadn't yet played out. People didn't go to that kind of trouble for the sake of a practical joke. Anyway, where were the laughs? Scaring people half to death just wasn't funny.

The paint stunt likely portended something else. What would come next?

3

In the midafternoon of the day of the paint attack, Hub convened a meeting in a Federal Building conference room. Members of the Joint FBI/NYPD Terrorism Task Force attended. In addition to Tina and Frank, the meeting included Mike Johannson, squad supervisor, and Danny Sussman, the NYPD representative.

A tape recorder was rolling on the conference table. From it issued a strangely pitched voice, a voice that a vo-corder had disguised. Specialty audio machines, vo-corders could make the most familiar voices unrecognizable.

The voice was saying, "Our first and last warning. We expect our demand to be met. There will be no negotiation. That is all."

The recording lapsed into silence. A moment passed. Then Tina asked, speaking the question in the minds of all present, "Demand for *what?* You hear any demand?"

Mike Johannson looked at Danny Sussman. "You sure this is all they got?"

Sussman nodded. "That's it," he said. A cop's cop, convex and bald, he'd won a spot on the coveted Terrorism Task Force owing to a long record of meticulous NYPD investigative work. At first he'd felt a bit out place teamed up with FBI people, whose Quantico training and federal outlook set them apart from the world of a precinct detective. Now, though, he felt at home. He played a crucial role: bridging the gap between two very different law-enforcement cultures.

Frank said offhandedly, "Maybe it's performance art."

Sussman sent Frank a charged glance. No matter how much he felt himself to be part of this team, Haddad's insouciant sense of humor still could get to him. Sometimes Frank just didn't seem serious about his job.

But his quip highlighted the fact that none of them had any idea why someone would inflict first terror, then blue paint, on a busful of ordinary commuters. They'd spent hours trying to puzzle it out. Apart from the inscrutable vo-corder message, phoned in to the NYPD from a Brooklyn pay phone, they'd come up with nothing.

Hub stood, and said, "Okay," his voice leading, demanding a response, an idea, anything that might prove useful. "Blue paint. Voice-altering technology . . ."

"Available from the Sharper Image catalogue," Frank cut in.

Sussman shot back, "Last I heard they weren't offering exploding paint bombs."

"Still," Hub said, a gesture calling Frank and Sussman to attention, "the rhetoric sounds political." He paused, glancing around the table. "Militia?"

"Not their style," Tina said crisply.

Hub looked at the one person there who might have insights into the probable perps. "Frank?"

Frank acknowledged the question with a nod. He knew what Hub had on his mind. And although he himself had been thinking it over, he wasn't entirely comfortable with the direction Hub wanted to go. He said, "Jihad isn't known for their sense of humor. And Hamas is raising so much money here, why queer their deal?"

Tina interjected, "Anyway, isn't green the color of Islam, not blue?"

The comment galvanized Frank. "And excuse me," he said, his voice tinged with exasperation, "but why do we immediately assume they're Arabs?"

Hub went into leadership mode, deflecting the

objections from Tina and Frank. "I want a composite of the suspects in circulation by the end of business today," he said brusquely. "Tina, you cross-check it against the mainframe. Mike, have you got the lab analysis on the paint?"

"Not yet," Mike Johannson replied.

Hub said, "See if any was sold in quantity the last month. Danny—" Tina's cell phone buzzed. As she answered it, Hub continued, "Find out what stop these guys got on the bus, maybe there's a witness."

"Hub," Frank said, his tone of voice gaining Hub's attention, interrupting the stream of instructions. "I think we're all eager to give up our weekends on this. It just occurs to me, has anybody even committed a crime here? I mean, assault with a deadly color?"

Hub didn't take umbrage. "Here's what I don't like," he declared. "They know explosives. They know our response time. They put in a call, and *walk*."

The others pondered that set of facts. Hub had a point. Though the paint bombers' objectives were baffling and their methods eccentric, they had executed the operation with finesse. That suggested training. Which, in turn, suggested sponsorship. Somebody was bankrolling this. And even if the somebody hadn't yet spelled it out, he had a specific objective: "We expect our demand to be met."

A young agent, Fred Darius, entered the room, holding a sheet of paper. "Excuse me, sir," he said to Hub. "I think you should see this. Came in on the fax."

Hub took the sheet of paper. Two words were printed on it: RELEASE HIM.

Hub blinked. "Release him?" he asked, not understanding what this meant. "Him who? Who are we holding?"

"Marv Albert?" Tina suggested, a wry glint in her eyes.

Danny Sussman said speculatively, "McVeigh?" Sussman thought of another possibility. "Sheik what's-his-name from the Trade Center?"

"Omar Abdel Rahman," Frank said, identifying the man Sussman had in mind. "Asshole," Frank added with contempt.

Fred Darius said, a bit diffidently on account of his junior status: "The Hamas guy got released in April."

"Under protest," Frank remarked.

Hub stared at the fax. "Why be coy about it?" he asked, unable to fathom the intent behind the two words. He wondered if the vagueness served a purpose. Was the sender trying to foment internal distrust? Could the message be telling Hub there was a whole lot he didn't know—that others in the U.S. law-enforcement hierarchy did know, but weren't sharing?

"You think it's phony?" Sussman inquired.

Tina Osu, meanwhile, had been conducting a low-pitched conversation on her cell phone. She covered the receiver, straightened, and said, "Hub, somebody's flashing a government badge over at the warehouse where they're working on the bus. Our tech guys want to know if we're cooperating with any other agencies on this thing."

Puzzlement drained from Hub's eyes. He gazed at Tina, his mind racing. Whoever was demanding the release of the mysterious "him" could take a back burner for the moment; anyway, Hub felt confident that the fax's sender would soon make himself more clearly understood. A bigger issue had just occupied the forefront of his attention. Somebody was messing with his case. Messing with his crime scene.

That would not do.

4

It was getting on toward the flinty dusk of wintertime New York as Hub and Frank Haddad drove across the East River to an old warehouse in Brooklyn. The building was providing a temporary garage for the waylaid #99 bus, and an ad hoc laboratory for a small army of Task Force technicians.

Agent Floyd Rose of the FBI, a tall African-American man who provided street-savvy investigative work for the Terrorism Task Force, waited at the entrance. The look on his face portended trouble. Rose told Hub tersely, "She's looking for wiring signatures on the device and asking for copies of any latent prints we've managed to lift."

Hub hadn't yet gotten a fix on the badge-wielding official's bureaucratic identity. A female with a fair degree of chutzpah, that was about all he knew. "Agency?" he asked Floyd Rose.

"Smells like it," Rose replied. "Turns out she's

also been talking to some of the passengers."

Task Force business occasionally had brought Hub into contact with one arm or another of the CIA. The encounters hadn't always been helpful. Often, in fact, they'd created problems that outweighed the payoffs. CIA people tended to have a one-way attitude about pooling resources; they expected full cooperation from the FBI, but resisted reciprocating the favor. Moreover, Hub suspected that any given CIA arm frequently didn't know what other arms were doing, a situation that hindered getting results in the shadowland called terrorism. For starters, it further confused the inevitable turf disputes between the two principal American law-and-order empires.

Hub led the way through the warehouse door. The interior, ordinarily dusty and decrepit, home to cobwebs and rusting junk, had undergone a transformation at odds with the building's unremarkable facade. The bus sat in a blinding bath of klieg lights. Technicians wearing white lab coats were subjecting it to different forensics procedures—fingerprint dusting, materials analysis, blast-vector reconstruction, human-tissue recovery. The technicians' concentration, and the beeps, buzzes, and hums of their machines, suggested that the bus contained a significance well beyond its history in public transportation.

Hub didn't recognize two of the technicians.

Freelancers? he wondered. *Brought in by whom?*

A youngish woman with a clipboard, also a stranger, seemed in charge. Her helmet of red hair framed a pretty, sharp-featured face; she sported a serious suit that the average government salary couldn't have begun to cover. Hub saw at a glance that this woman didn't often take no as an answer. She looked up as he approached.

"Hi," Hub said neutrally.

The woman studied him. "Hi, there," she said, her voice equally undemonstrative.

"Special Agent Anthony Hubbard," Hub informed her. "FBI."

"Oh, shit," the woman exclaimed. "I've been trying to liaise with you all day!" She seemed sincere; friendly, too. "My name is Elise Kraft," she went on. "National Security Council." With disarming poise, she extended her hand for a shake, every inch a senior professional, pleased to meet a colleague of perhaps not-quite-equal rank.

Hub didn't take her hand. He said slowly, "And you've been trying to 'liaise' with me all day?" Though courteous, Hub was drawing a line. "Did you think of trying the phone book, Elise? We have fourteen lines, that's not counting the unlisted ones."

Her arm still extended, her hand still inviting a shake, Elise said unflappably, "Hi, I'm Elise Kraft, National Security Council."

Hub didn't react. He just gazed at her. Though Frank Haddad and Floyd Rose watched with impassive stares, and the technicians stayed focused on their work, a strain field was developing in the warehouse. All present felt it: Something would break.

Hub finally took Elise Kraft's hand. But after shaking it he didn't let go; he looked Elise in the eye, and declared, "And *I'm* Colin Powell."

Elise didn't blink, Frank noticed. Either she had no sense of humor or understood that Hub didn't buy the NSC cover story.

Hub demanded, "What exactly do you people want with my bus?"

Elise tried to disengage her hand. Hub tightened his grip. The strain around them ratcheted up in intensity; even the technicians stopped pretending to ignore it.

"We're all on the same team here, Agent Hubbard," Elise said evenly. But with a note of developing irritation.

"Who *exactly*," Hub inquired, "is 'we' on this particular team, Elise?"

"It's never the question that's indiscreet," Elise remarked with aplomb, as if she'd come up with an epigrammatic gem. "Only the answer."

Hub smiled and released Elise's hand, apparently enjoying the adroit way she had sidestepped his search for information. Elise returned the smile, her eyes brightening with approval. But her estimation of Hub hadn't risen, Hub knew. On the contrary—Elise thought she'd charmed the Special Agent into refraining from awkward questions. So it went with CIA operatives. Especially, of course, with the pretty ones.

But Elise Kraft could not have been more mistaken. Hub said breezily, "Tell you what. You send me an official interagency request for cooperation on this, and I'll give you copies of everything we come up with. Otherwise," he went on, his voice developing an edge, "get your ass on out of here before you contaminate my crime scene any more than you already have."

Elise's gaze held steady. "There's no reason to be nasty," she said.

Hub's eyes widened, mock-surprised. "You think *this* is nasty?" He gave her a big smile, his version of interagency charm. "In case you haven't heard," he went on, "the CIA has no charter to operate domestically. Which puts you in violation of federal law."

Elise didn't back off. "Not according to the Cooperation Agreement, Special Order 12333—I suggest you reread the paragraph on sharing information. I happen to be well within my authority."

Hub's eyebrows rose. "Special Order 12333 refers to domestic terrorism," he pointed out. "You got something you want to 'share' with me?"

Elise didn't reply. She just stared at him.

"Us being teammates and all?" Hub prodded.

Elise held up her clipboard. "Unfortunately, not yet," she replied, shaking her head. "But as soon as I do, I'll—"

"Get back to me, yeah, I know," Hub said with the skepticism of one who has heard it before. His hand closed on the clipboard, plucking it from Elise's grasp. "Here's what I'm going to do," he continued, his manner no-nonsense now, forbidding dissent. "I'm gonna have a couple of my 'teammates' here escort you back to wherever you came from. And then I'm gonna go back to the office and wait for that official cooperation request." His eyes bored into hers. "Okay by you?"

Through clenched teeth, Elise said, "Swell."

"Nice meeting you, Elise," Hub remarked. "Is that Elise with an 'E' or an 'A'?"

Elise said coolly, her poise intact, "Nice meeting you, too, Special Agent Hubbard."

They gazed at each other a few moments more. Then Frank Haddad and Floyd Rose escorted Elise to the door. Hub followed them out.

Two agents stood near the entrance. Hub watched Frank give them instructions, then watched Elise's retreating backside as she was led away into the twilight's shadows.

Hub turned to Floyd Rose. "Tail her," he said bluntly.

5

That night Frank and his wife, Najiba, hosted a gathering at their home to celebrate the day their son, Frank Jr., had finished reading the Holy Koran. Haddad family members and friends filled the tastefully appointed living room, dressed to the hilt in observance of the importance of the occasion. Hub was there as well, looking respectful, along with the rest of Frank Sr.'s close Task Force colleagues.

The guests listened to thirteen-year-old Frank Jr. perform a ritual declaration. The dark-haired lad's good looks echoed those of his parents, despite suffering the temporary burden of braces. He recited solemnly in Arabic:

"In the Name of Allah, the beneficent, the merciful. Say: I seek refuge in the Lord of Men, the King of Men.'"

Frank Jr. did a nice job with the recitation, even if, unlike his parents, his Arabic lacked the fluency of those who grew up speaking it as a native tongue.

The boy's theological teacher offered a final benediction. As he spoke, also in Arabic, the Muslim guests covered their faces with their hands:

"*'Make me know that which I have become ignorant of; and make me recite it in the hours of the night and the day; and make it an argument for me O Thou Sustainer of all the worlds!' Ameen!*"

To which all assembled replied, "*Ameen.*"

Frank Jr. flashed a broad smile at his parents. For once, now that he had cleared a hurdle that the Haddads took seriously, he didn't feel bashful about his braces. Frank and Najiba beamed back at him, portraits of pride.

Some minutes later the guests helped themselves to a sumptuous spread of Middle Eastern pastries and sweet tea. A buzz of conversation filled the apartment, a mixture of accented English, American English, and voluble Arabic.

Hub ambled up to Tina Osu. She remarked, "Nice, wasn't it?"

"Very," Hub said quietly. The ceremony had impressed him. He'd always had a thing for close-knit families, and for the power of faith that so often sustained such families. This appreciation had intensified over the last few years as he himself, for one reason or another, mostly having to do with his preoccupation with work, hadn't managed to start a family of his own.

A moment of silence fell between him and Tina.

Tina gave him a glance. And said, "You ever gonna stop by, pick up your things?"

Hub nodded but didn't comment. In these surroundings especially, he wanted to avoid that particular topic. It reminded him of his bachelor status, of the fact that he lacked not only matrimonial prospects, but casual romance as well. His affair with Tina, at first a romp but ultimately a case of no common ground, was only the latest example.

Several feet away, Mike Johannson and Danny Sussman kept an eye on the interaction between Hub and Tina. Danny cleared his throat. "He doing her?" he asked Mike *sotto voce*.

"Some detective you are," Mike replied. "They stopped."

Fred Darius, passing by, overheard the exchange. "Really?" he said. He glanced longingly at Tina. "I wonder if she likes white guys."

Danny shared Fred's sentiments from a slightly different perspective. He said, "I wonder if she likes bald guys."

The three agents watched Hub cross the room to Najiba Haddad.

"You must be so proud," Hub told her with feeling.

Najiba smiled. "Small children," she said philo-sophically, "small worries. Big children . . ."

"Big orthodontia bills," her husband Frank interrupted, singling out one of the bigger worries. In fact, Frank felt lucky to be able to count dental work as a filial problem. Back in Lebanon, his own parents hadn't been nearly as fortunate; they'd raised Frank amid mortar explosions, midnight raids, fanatic ravings on the street, and Israeli counterattacks. Luckily, though, all that now belonged to the distant past. Frank grinned, glad to be master of a domain over which Hub held no sway. He told his boss with a degree of irony, "Someday, you'll understand."

Hub nodded, wondering about that. He didn't know if he ever would understand. If he'd ever get the chance.

Frank noticed a man standing in the front entrance: Hub's driver. Evidently the ASAC's work-day hadn't come to a close. "Where we going?" Frank asked him, a touch of apprehension in his voice.

"You're staying with your family," Hub replied, moving toward the door. "I'm back in the morn-ing."

Frank watched Hub take his leave, curious how the boss did it. Devotion to the job was one thing. Marriage to it was something else altogether.

6

Early the next morning Hub passed through the Federal Building's security checkpoints, then through the FBI's guarded lobby on the twenty-second floor. He entered his office, a self-contained area with secretarial space out front, unoccupied at the moment owing to Janeen's long-standing refusal to show up until at least eight. The office was bigger and nicer than the cubicles through which Hub had wended his way to the FBI's senior ranks. It seemed like home. In most respects, it *was* home.

A pile of surveillance photos, the overnight production of Floyd Rose's surveillance crew, waited on the desk. The subject: Elise Kraft, crime-scene meddler and bombshell spook.

At least that was what Hub figured her to be. The photos didn't tell him much. Elise seemed to live a fairly unflamboyant life. Nice apartment building, nice car, a close relationship with her cell phone, no apparent office.

So she really was a spook. Curiously, though, Hub hadn't yet seen a formal interagency cooperation request. If Elise was such hot stuff at the CIA, how come she hadn't rustled one up? She shouldn't have had a problem with that. When it came to top Agency people, the FBI routinely fulfilled overnight requests.

Hub could only conclude that Elise had reasons to keep a low profile. Was she not pulling the usual strings because she wanted to keep something quiet? The possibility made Hub wary. One thing seemed for sure. Elise wouldn't willingly share her agenda with him.

Not a problem, Hub told himself. If things heated up, and went too far in the wrong direction without a formal documentation of Elise's legitimacy—well, in that case she would have to share her agenda *unwillingly*.

Someone entered the office. Frank Haddad; Hub knew from the way the man breathed. Frank's lightly accented voice asked, "You sleep here?"

Hub smiled, but didn't look up.

"Immigration called," Frank added.

Hub stretched and stood. A development was breaking. Frank's tone made that clear.

*　　*　　*

The Immigration and Naturalization Service kept offices in the Federal Building on floors eight through ten. Hub and Frank took the elevator down, stepped into the INS reception area, and showed their badges to the guard. Like the FBI, INS had reasons to maintain rigorous security. That hadn't always been the case. Not too many years before, pizza guys and bicycle messengers had been free to roam hallways, even offices, to make deliveries. Even tourists used to drop in to ask for directions. No longer. Costly experience had shown that until proved otherwise, all visitors had to be deemed potential threats.

Frank led Hub to a holding area. It resembled a miniature penitentiary. Barred cells lined two walls, passageways were heavily gated, uniformed officers manned a central checkpoint equipped with security monitors. After the FBI agents signed in, the duty officer buzzed them through a gate. They walked along the passage beyond to a door. Frank opened it. They entered a narrow, dim room with a big plate-glass window to one side. A surveillance gallery.

Beyond the window lay a small room. A dark-skinned man, simply dressed, haggard, and obviously quite scared, sat at a table. A uniformed official stood over him asking sharply worded questions. Speakers carried the interrogation into the surveillance gallery; Hub listened, noting that significant language issues were getting in the way. The detainee and the interrogator couldn't see the observers. From their vantage point the window was a mirror.

An INS supervisor in civilian clothes entered the surveillance gallery carrying a suitcase. Hub watched him open a false bottom. Under it a large quantity of cash reposed in neat stacks.

"All in small bills," the INS man explained. "So we figure, smurf, right? Then I think, considering the gentleman's nationality, plus where he's been recently, we better call Frank."

"Who's trying to score points with his boss," Frank said blithely. "Big-time."

Hub asked with a thoughtful frown, "Has he broken any laws?"

"No, sir," the INS man said. "He's twenty bucks under the $10,000 limit."

Frank extracted his wallet and produced a twenty. "Not anymore," he declared. Hub gave him a look; bending rules wasn't his style, never had been. Frank knew that. He acknowledged the look with an innocent smile.

Behind the window, the interrogator seemed to think that volume might overcome the language barrier. He bellowed, "So, Khalil—you're saying this is an *inheritance*? Somebody *died* and you're bringing them the *money*?"

Khalil cringed, trying to keep up despite being

more scared and confused than ever. "No, no," he stammered. *"Dhouri . . ."*

Frank said to Hub, "He means 'dowry.'"

"Check out his neck," Hub murmured.

Small puckered scars disfigured Khalil's neck. The wounds hadn't healed well; they resembled tiny craters. The INS man gave them a puzzled stare.

"The tabac," Frank said, unpleasant memories surfacing from his childhood. He took a puff from an imaginary cigarette, then held out an arm and pretended to extinguish the cigarette on it. "Sssssss," Frank hissed, evoking the sound of sizzling flesh. "The territories."

Hub pondered the significance of that. Khalil here seemed to have had a checkered past. That implied a checkered future, as did the suitcase's hidden cash. He might not know a whole lot. But he could be doing business with someone who did.

Hub came to a decision. "Put him in play," he said.

Forty minutes later Hub and Frank were roaring down the Van Wyck Expressway in a rental Contour. Frank drove while Hub used a cell phone. They were tailing Khalil, who occupied a cab not far ahead.

Hub loudly told his phone, "On the Van Wyck . . . No, not yet." He turned to Frank, and asked, "What are we in?"

"A '97 Contour," Frank replied. "On *my* credit card." He glowered at the cab they were following. "Back home," he grumbled, "the security services'd be up this guy's ass with a poker. But what do we do, we let him go."

Not quite, thought Hub, who was improvising plans off the top of his head. "Six teams on the ground, at least," he said to the phone." He listened a moment. Then he added impatiently, "Well, pull 'em off the UN!" Frank's driving distracted him; they'd come closer to the cab. "Stay back," he admonished.

Frank shook his head, feeling a little stung. "Not my first date, Hub," he pointed out. Ahead, the cab changed lanes, apparently preparing to exit. Onto the Brooklyn-Queens Expressway, Frank learned from the off-ramp's sign. "He's taking the BQE," he announced. "Looks like it's Brooklyn."

Hub brayed into the phone, "I want husbands and wives, I want baby carriages, and no Brooks Brothers. He's headed for Brooklyn. Pass the word to Kew Gardens," he added, referring to the Bureau's Brooklyn office.

"You're micromanaging," Frank informed his boss.

Hub paid him no mind. "And find me a judge I can work with. We want sound on this guy . . . *damn* . . . I'm losing you!" He raised his voice further. "*And bring us a radio!*"

Frank pitied the agents on the receiving end of Hub's stream of instructions. Hell, Frank felt sorry for himself. The ASAC didn't usually launch a complex operation on the spur of the moment. That was because the ASAC usually had little tolerance for ambiguous loose ends. At the moment, however, a whole lot of Brooklyn loose ends were coming right at them, threatening to swallow a courier who Frank would bet his right arm was up to no good. As in, carrying seed money for people with unpeaceful plans. Frank considered asking Hub to take a deep breath and think things through. Instead he said, a bit nervously, "I get reimbursed for this, right?"

The cab stopped in a low-rent district on Atlantic Avenue. The area looked like an amalgamation of Kinshasa, Beirut, Tel Aviv, and Moscow. A Third World polyglot of diverse cultures, its atmosphere seemed volatile, liable to suddenly combust. How could one place contain people who babbled a multitude of mutually antagonistic languages—Arabic, Hebrew, esoteric dialects of the former Soviet Union, the former Zaire?

While a full answer to that question could have been debated at length, and indeed often was, Brooklynites agreed on a favorite short answer: hope. Despite the diversity and the historic animosities, or perhaps because of them, Atlantic

Avenue teemed with vitality. It didn't matter that storefront signs were handwritten in scripts that only minorities could read. Commerce thrived anyway; oranges were oranges, halvah was halvah, and tea was tea, commodities that could be haggled over in the universal lingo of dollars and cents. An old American story, one that had played out again and again, between the Irish and the Italians, the Norwegians and the Germans, the New England Pilgrims and the Maryland Catholics. Although, to be sure, rarely if ever had the American melting pot been so complexly larded as late-nineties Brooklyn.

Hub and Frank watched Khalil pay the cab driver, then set off on foot.

Frank pulled the Contour to the curb a safe distance behind. He had a feel for neighborhoods like this, having grown up in variants of it. An olive-skinned youth walked by with a boom box throbbing out *"Oum Khatoum,"* the latest in neo-Palestinian techno-rock. Frank wondered if Frank Jr. might like the tune; he made a mental note to pick up a disc. Maybe he'd turn the kid onto a current version of the family roots. . . .

No time to think about that now. An agent approached Hub's window and slipped in a walkie-talkie. Hub immediately put it to use. Meanwhile, a man carrying groceries took up position behind Khalil: Fred Darius, dressed-down from his usual business clothes. He paused as Khalil suddenly turned into a storefront.

Frank watched Khalil buy a Coke and a Baby Ruth bar. "Twelve bucks in Gaza," he remarked to Hub.

"America's the place to be if you're a terrorist," Hub replied tersely. He keyed the walkie-talkie, and told it, "Fred's hovering. Patsy, take over."

Fred Darius slipped away. A woman pushing a stroller replaced him. Pedestrians blocked Frank's view; he got out of the Contour to keep Khalil in sight. He hadn't left the store. Frank started to get back in the car, then noticed that Hub had moved to behind the wheel.

The boss wanted to drive. Frank couldn't argue with that. He walked around and opened the passenger-side door. Hub's cell phone, on the seat, rang as he entered. Frank answered it. An authoritative voice asked for Anthony Hubbard. "Who's calling?" Frank asked.

"Abraham Frankel," the voice replied.

"I got the judge," Frank said as he passed the phone to Hub.

"Good morning, sir," Hub said to the phone. "How're things in the Second Circuit this morning?" Hub listened a moment, a smile tugging at the corners of his mouth. "I hear you," he said sympathetically. "Listen, Judge, we're in a kind of situation here . . ." Hub stopped short as he glimpsed Khalil exiting the store, then moving away down the sidewalk. "Hold on, will ya, Your Judge?"

Khalil paused. In the flux of pedestrian traffic, Hub made out a man standing next to him. Khalil appeared to be talking with the guy. Hub barked into the walkie-talkie, "Is he talking to somebody, who's he talking to? Are we *getting film?*"

Two hundred yards away, an agent with a telephoto lens got Khalil in close-up. He was chatting with a man whose café-au-lait complexion suggested a Palestinian background—a distinguished face, blessed with patrician good looks. The camera's motor drive clicked multiple times, capturing both faces.

In the Contour, Hub covered the cell phone's mouthpiece. "Frank?" he said, hoping for a make on the face.

Frank squinted at the sidewalk conversation. "Don't know him," he muttered. "If we were allowed to get sound on them, we'd know him," he added pointedly, reminding Hub that Judge Frankel, on the phone, could green-light audio surveillance.

The walkie-talkie crackled to life, confirming photos of Khalil conversing with the good-looking Palestinian. Hub covered the radio with one hand; his other hand returned the cell phone to his ear. Frank watched the two-fisted juggling act, apprehensive that Hub was trying to deal with too much all at once.

"What's that?" Hub asked the cell phone. "No, Judge, not yet we're not—but we have reason to believe he may be involved with—" Out of the corner of an eye Hub noticed that a member of one of his undercover teams was looking a tad too conspicuous. Trying too hard to blend in, not trying hard enough to veil his scrutiny of Khalil and the Palestinian gentleman. Hub slapped a hand over the cell phone again, keyed the walkie-talkie, and yelled, "Damn it, Tommy!" Then he jerked his head at Frank. "He's overacting! Tell him—" Judge Frankel was waiting, Hub remembered. "Sorry, Judge," he told the cell phone. "No . . ." Hub grimaced. "I just . . ."

Frank exclaimed softly, "He's making him. Shit. Fuck. He's . . ."

Khalil's face was undergoing a subtle transformation. Frank knew the look. It derived from a sixth sense that life on the West Bank engendered, an ability to intuit from tiny, disparate clues that enemies had infiltrated a seemingly ordinary scene. Khalil froze. What came next didn't surprise Frank at all. Khalil broke into a headlong dash.

Hub mashed walkie-talkie keys, and shouted, "*Go, go, go! All units, go!*" Then he dropped both the walkie-talkie and the cell phone, slammed the car into gear, and laid rubber as he peeled out into traffic. Horns blared.

Six different surveillance teams broke cover,

dropping all pretense to be shopping or gossiping or dog-walking or hawking wares, and sprinted after Khalil. Pedestrians gaped. Khalil, spooked, went into overdrive. Cars weaved to avoid him and came to abrupt halts, brakes screeching. Pedestrian traffic stilled as people turned to stare.

Hub hurtled down the street in pursuit. Ahead, double-parked cars on either side left a narrow gap in the street's middle. Hub went for it. He jammed the Contour through, scraping both sides. The metallic rasp wasn't music to Frank's ears. Cringing, he yelled, *"Christ!"*

Hub groped for the cell phone. "Judge," he snapped into it. "I'm gonna have to call you back."

Khalil bolted into a crowded open-air market and immediately collided with several veiled women carrying bags full of produce. The women went down, fruits and vegetables sailing through the air. Vendors' stalls blocked Khalil's way. He vaulted over one after another, sending cascades of merchandise to the ground. Angry salespeople protested, then fell silent as they perceived a second, bigger onslaught coming at them—Hub and Frank in the Contour, dozens of madly running agents in unraveling disguises. Hub swerved the Contour into an alley, hoping to cut off Khalil's escape route, in the process raking a line of parked cars. Metal crumpled, side mirrors snapped, windows cracked. *"Shit!"* Frank exclaimed, resisting an urge to clap his hands over his eyes. "Didn't take the insurance!"

For a moment it looked as if Hub had succeeded in cornering Khalil. But just then a soccer ball bounced into his peripheral vision. Something was following it. Two young boys—headed directly for the Contour's path. . . .

Hub veered away, slamming the car into the alley's wall but sparing the kids. They stared at him, wide-eyed, speechless, as their ball rolled away. Hub, poker-faced, nodded at them. Then he flung open his door and lit out after Khalil on foot.

Frank inspected the wall that had jammed his door permanently shut. Cursing under his breath, he scrambled across the seat to the driver-side door, popped out, and took off after Hub.

The ASAC, his arms and legs pumping with the vigor of a twenty-year-old, his dark overcoat flapping, gained on Khalil. Then something unexpected joined the action.

A van sped down the alley toward Khalil, its side doors sliding open, two pairs of hands reaching out. From nowhere a man appeared. He bodychecked Khalil, sent him careening into the van, and jumped in after him. The doors clanged shut; with the howl rubber makes when applied liberally to pavement, the van shot out of the alley, barged through traffic, and disappeared.

Hub stared after it, panting, his fists clenched.

Frank ran up, also panting. "Damn," he gasped. "*Shit!*"

"Yeah," Hub said quietly. "Yeah."

Ten minutes later Hub presided over an impromptu huddle in the alley. Agents gathered around him, their radios making a racket. Overhead, helicopters circled.

Fred Darius spoke up, his youthful face drawn. "They just found the van. Doesn't look like they're gonna find any fingerprints."

Hub nodded. Par for the course in this game; everything had blown up in his face. Not far away, the agent who'd taken telephoto pictures activated a digital printer in an unmarked car. A photo slid forth. The agent brought it to Hub: a clear shot of Khalil and the handsome Palestinian.

"Run him down, bring him in," Hub ordered wearily.

Fred Darius's cell phone buzzed. He answered it and exchanged a few words with the caller. Then he handed the phone to Hub. "Floyd Rose," Fred explained.

"Go, Floyd," Hub said into the phone. As he listened, a smile spread slowly across his face.

7

Hub drove his unmarked car through a Brooklyn neighborhood of modest, neatly maintained homes, and pulled to the curb not far from a house—the address of which Floyd Rose had supplied. Nothing about the area to arouse suspicion of any kind: a man walking his dog, a Plymouth parked on the street with two people in it, trees, brown grass, the wails of a small child trickling from an open window. A sleepy neighborhood under the morning sun.

The passenger-side door opened. Floyd Rose got in and settled his tall frame. He told Hub, "I got two in the Plymouth, at least three inside, and see that guy walking his dog? It did its business about an hour ago, and they're still walking."

Hub nodded, glancing at another unmarked Bureau car parked down the street. It held Frank Haddad and Danny Sussman.

They, too, had taken note of the fellow walking his dog. Danny remarked, "I had a dog like that once."

Frank snorted. "It's not *his* dog, numb-nuts. They're spies."

Danny blinked with mock-naïveté. "The dog works for the CIA?"

Frank was about to reply when his radio came alive with Hub's voice: "All units report in turn."

A series of acknowledgments came over the air:

"Unit One is good to go."

"Unit Two, we're ready to rock."

"Unit Three all set."

Frank told his radio, "Unit Four is go."

"Let's roll," Hub declared.

Two pedestrians had been conversing on the sidewalk. They confronted the dog-walker, double-teaming him before he could react. "Federal agents," Mike Johannson informed the guy. *"Hands behind your back."* The dog snarled, baring fangs. A third agent tossed his jacket over it.

Two unmarked cars meantime fishtailed across the quiet street. They boxed in the Plymouth; Fred Darius turned from the sidewalk, a 12-gauge Remington Pump emerging from his coat. He thrust the barrel through the driver's window, and said, "Keep 'em where we can see 'em, thank you very much." The guys in the Plymouth stared stonily at Fred. Not a thing they could do except choose to die.

Moments later an outsize custom shotgun blew in the house's front door. An industrial silencer muffled the barrel, muting the blast. Two men sat inside, gaping at the hole where the door had been, fork-equipped hands suspended over takeout they'd been munching. Frank Haddad and Tina Osu advanced on them, guns extended. Frank snapped, "Hi, guys, I expect you know the drill."

Hub's tall frame filled the destroyed doorway. He stepped in, his eyes roving. The place wasn't furnished. He moved warily from one empty room to the next, keeping his footfalls soft. More bare walls, more bare floors. He came to a stairway that led to the basement. Voices drifted up as he slowly descended, taking care to make no sound. Hub reached the bottom and froze. Khalil sat in a chair, looking like hell. Behind him stood a guy Hub remembered having seen working on the bus at the warehouse. And across from Khalil, in a BarcaLounger, her demeanor tougher and a touch less cute than when Hub first had encountered it, reclined none other than Elise Kraft.

The basement room differed from the upstairs rooms in a curious way. While it was furnished normally, in marked contrast to the rest of the house, it didn't strike Hub as a comfort zone. This hideaway rumpus room—Elise's private den—wasn't a place for relaxation and fun. On the contrary. Hub far preferred the emptiness above.

He stepped forward, revealing himself. The man standing behind Khalil pointed a 9mm Glock at his head. Hub didn't flinch. He simply stared the guy down.

Elise drawled, "Ralph, spare us."

The gun lowered. Hub studied Khalil; his face was badly bruised. The man had taken a shellacking.

"I never touched him," Elise said airily.

"Really?" Hub inquired. "I'm taking him into custody just the same."

"What are you going to charge him with?" Elise demanded. "Jaywalking?" Hub stared at her. Elise stared back; in measured tones, she said, "I don't suppose we could just have a little chat with him here first?"

"Not in this lifetime," Hub said softly.

"You know, Hub," Elise remarked with expansive self-assurance. "May I call you Hub?" She didn't wait for a reply; instead she went on conversationally, "If you guys hadn't blown the surveillance, we'd have been able to follow the money. What do you think, Khalil—you would have led us right to your friends, wouldn't you?"

Khalil shuddered, unable to look in her direction.

"What friends?" Hub asked, his voice leading, demanding a reply. "What have you got for me, Elise?" He paused. "Enlighten me." Elise's face remained opaque. "Tell me now," Hub added. "Or tell me downtown."

Elise said nothing. She simply stared from the BarcaLounger, unperturbed, as if expecting someone to bring her a drink.

"People," Hub called up the stairs. Agents clattered down the steps into the room. "Get this guy out of here and book him."

Agents advanced on Khalil.

Elise said, "One phone call and he's mine again. You know the number. I have—"

Hub barked, "*You have* the right to remain silent. *You have* the right to an attorney. Anything you say *can* and *will* be held against you *in a court of law . . .*"

"Oh come *on*," Elise interrupted, her voice rising. "Do you have any idea what you're starting here, the kind of shitstorm you're about to . . ."

"Kidnapping," Hub snapped, cutting her off. "Obstruction of justice. *Assault*." He wheeled away, headed for the stairs. "Cuff her," he told a waiting agent.

Minutes later, handcuffed, Elise sat in the rear of Hub's car. Frank drove. Hub sat beside him. "So, Elise," Frank called. "You okay back there, you don't get carsick or anything? Those handcuffs too tight?"

Elise didn't react to the taunts. She said pensively, "Shouf Mountains, right? Shiite or Sunni?"

Frank did an astonished double take in the rearview mirror. "Wow," he exclaimed quietly. "You're really good." He glanced at Hub. "She's really good," he informed his boss.

If Frank's assessment impressed Hub, he kept it to himself. He turned to look at Elise. "You ready to tell us what's going on here, Elise? Was the paint bomb a warning?"

Elise ignored the questions. She asked Frank, "American University of Beirut? I was there from '79 to '82."

"No shit?" Frank said. Again he glanced a Hub.

"My father taught economics," Elise went on. "Henry Kraft?"

Hub said impatiently, "Is there a terrorist cell operating in this city that we're unaware of?"

Elise continued to ignore him. "Such a tragedy," Elise remarked to Frank. "Growing up in that city was . . ." She paused, her eyes nostalgically aglow. "Paradise. Like an exotic Paris, wasn't it, Frank?"

Hub said, "You ever been in Rikers, Elise? You know what happens there?"

Finally Elise favored Hub with a gaze. Not a hint of fear in it; Hub might have suggested a stop to get hot fudge sundaes. "Yum," she said tranquilly.

Frank wondered if anything could faze this woman.

Then his beeper went off.

*   *   *

It looked like every cop car in Brooklyn had converged on the scene. Lights flashing, they ringed a wide downtown intersection near the waterfront, almost in the shadow of the Brooklyn Bridge. SWAT teams deployed along the rooftops of neighboring buildings, agile figures with high-powered rifles— a sight more associated with the Yugoslavian civil war than with nineties America. Sharpshooters knocked on the doors of the area's upper-floor apartments, seeking permission to take positions at windows, politely slipping in even when residents couldn't summon words to give permission. Shocked families acquiesced. Mothers herded frightened children to inner rooms.

The object of this attention stood in the middle of the intersection: a #87 bus, alone in an expanse of bare pavement. The scopes trained on it revealed terrified passengers standing in the aisle. They obscured other people, shadowy figures responsible for the standoff. Unlike the #99 bus, these hijackers had remained on board.

Frank drove Hub's car to the perimeter of the police cordon. Hub stepped out, caught sight of the NYPD officer in charge, and approached him.

"Definitely Arab types," the officer explained. His badge identified him as Sergeant Flamini. "Only this time they're still in there."

"Any communication at all?" Hub asked.

"Nope," Flamini said. He shrugged. "It's weird. They're just *in* there."

Hub said, "Get the frequency of the driver's radio and patch it through to this number." Hub scribbled down his cell phone's number, handed it to the sergeant. "We need two lines." He turned to Frank. "Frank, get a negotiator out here."

Frank pulled out his cell phone. Another cop was standing by. He spoke up. "Sir, they've got kids in there. We count six."

Hub winced, a knot tightening in his stomach. He accessed experience, training, and will, and shut down his emotions. Kids on the bus; he considered the fact strategically. "That gives us something to work with," he announced. He walked back to his car.

Elise leaned forward as he opened the driver's door. "What's happening out there?" she asked.

Hub didn't reply.

"They've taken another bus, haven't they?" Elise persisted. "Talk to me."

Hub said coldly, "Oh, *now* you want to talk. You want to be my friend, is that it?"

"Listen," Elise said earnestly. "These guys are the real deal."

"How do *you* know?" Hub demanded.

Elise stared with her stonewall look.

Hub exclaimed, "Is there a terrorist cell operating in Brooklyn?"

Four seconds ticked by. Then Elise said, "Yes."

Like pulling teeth, Hub thought. *But at least she's starting to open up.* "Was the blue paint a warning?" he asked.

"Yes," replied Elise. She looked quite worried; not faking it, Hub decided. She added, "And I'm afraid this time they'll blow the bus."

Sirens spiraled through the hazy daylight. Fire trucks rumbled down side streets; ambulances formed an outer ring beyond the cop cars. Hub said, his eyes hard, "If they wanted to blow the bus, then why haven't they blown the bus?"

Elise said, "I . . ." She shook her head. "I don't know."

Hub turned on his heel and walked away.

"Agent Hubbard," Elise called. "Please. Maybe I can help."

Hub didn't look back. He strode a short distance to a hastily improvised command post behind a SWAT van. Frank stood there with Sergeant Flamini. He said to Hub, "The driver's name is Larry Kaiser. He says they've got explosives strapped to their chests, they got automatic weapons, and they're speaking Arabic." While Frank wasn't happy about any of those circumstances, the last one hit home in a personal way.

Elise watched from the car, trying to catch every word.

"Where the hell's the negotiator?" Hub demanded.

Frank said tensely, "Tunnels got twenty-minute delays, and they're working on both bridges."

Hub turned to Sergeant Flamini. "What else did he say about the device? Did he describe it at all? Anything about a button, or a cord, or . . ." He broke off as a freshly arrived vehicle parked just beyond the police perimeter. It didn't belong to any of the city's emergency fleets. Technicians got out and began erecting a satellite-dish tower: an ENG truck. The first representatives of the broadcast media had hit the scene.

From the car came a low gasp: "Oh, God."

Frank looked at Elise. Her face had gone pale. Frank glanced at Hub; conferring with cops, he hadn't heard Elise's gasp. Something was bothering the woman. She said, "They're not here to negotiate."

"Meaning?" Frank demanded.

"They're waiting for the cameras."

The idea jolted Frank. "Hub," he said, interrupting the ASAC's conversation. Hub looked up. Frank nodded at Elise, inviting her to repeat what she had just said.

Elise told Hub, "They want the newsies here. They want everybody watching."

Hub and Frank exchanged glances. If Elise was

onto something, they had much less time than they'd imagined. Maybe no time at all.

"You've got the shooters in place?" Elise asked.

"So?" Frank said.

"Use 'em," Elise said emphatically.

"What?" Hub said blankly.

"Kill 'em now," Elise replied.

Hub and Frank stared at her. Wondering what she knew that they didn't.

Sergeant Flamini was listening in. He said to Hub, "I got the marksmen on the com. They're looking for a clean shot." He spoke into his radio, asking for status reports.

Two more news vans pulled up to the perimeter. TV reporters emerged, instantly recognizable. Technicians rapidly assembled video and audio gear. Hub watched from a corner of his eye. A media circus was building.

Sergeant Flamini clapped a hand over his radio's mouthpiece. "Shooter says they've got the passengers all standing in the aisle," he reported. "He says, 'No go.'"

Hub studied Elise. Her eyes held a genuine emotion; dread, Hub realized. She truly expected the worst. More seconds ticked by. Overhead, the air filled with the *thump* of an approaching helicopter. Hub glanced at it. Not one, but two choppers had arrived. Logos identified them as the skycams of local television stations. Rivals in the current ratings wars, they dueled aggressively for optimal position above the standoff.

Hub took a deep breath. He said to Flamini and a number of other cops who had gathered, "We have rules of engagement we're gonna follow here, folks, so put the safeties back on your weapons." He shot Elise a look. "Nobody's killing anybody until we see what's what."

Elise chewed a lip. Frank knew she wanted to press her case. Handcuffed, however, she couldn't argue from a position of authority. Just as well, Frank decided. At the same time, he had a feeling that the CIA agent may have put her finger on the reality of the situation. If the men holding the bus truly were the "real deal"—not amateurs staging a half-baked stunt—they wouldn't hesitate to splatter themselves to kingdom come. People like that were capable of the most extreme measures imaginable in pursuit of a valuable goal. And it did seem to Frank that a big play in the news might help achieve their goal.

As things stood, the terrorists were already making a media splash. And as for their ultimate goal—the "Release him" demand notwithstanding, Frank couldn't begin to guess what it might be. But Elise, he suspected, didn't have to guess. She knew.

The news teams kicked into high gear. Correspondents breathlessly served up live, on-the-spot reports, all of them attempting to impart greater drama than their rivals. *So it goes with terrorism,* Frank thought gloomily. The same script had been played out numerous times in Jerusalem, Cairo, London, Paris, and Rome.

Why did it have to come to Brooklyn?

8

Sergeant Flamini alerted Hub to the fact that two phone lines had been connected with the bus driver's radio. Hub keyed one line. Frank keyed the other.

With the negotiator and the translator held up in traffic, Hub couldn't afford to wait. It was time to talk to Larry Kaiser and, if possible, the men who had commandeered Kaiser's bus.

Hub told his phone in a strong, clear voice, "Larry, this is Agent Hubbard of the FBI. I'll be negotiating our way out of this. Let me talk to one of them . . ."

Kaiser interrupted, sounding shaky but in possession of his wits. He explained that the terrorists didn't seem to speak English.

"I know," Hub replied. "I know. You just hang in there, Larry. No, don't worry, I've got somebody here who can translate."

Hub looked at Frank. Both men heard Larry

Kaiser pass his radio to someone else. In the background a young boy was crying. A nervous female voice, low-pitched, tried to hush the child.

A steady breathing sound came over the line. "Sir," Hub said, "my name is Anthony Hubbard. I don't have any authority to make deals or respond to demands. I just want to find out if you need anything in there. If any of the passengers are in need of medical attention?"

Frank translated rapidly in fluent Arabic. When he finished Hub covered his mouthpiece. "Frank?" he said, hoping that Frank had picked up on something he'd missed.

His own mouthpiece covered, Frank replied, "I don't know if they understand."

Hub grimaced. He said into his phone, "Sir, is there anything you want to say to me? That I can tell my people here?"

Frank translated. Then he stared at Hub, and said, "The guy's just breathing into the phone. Maybe they're not even Arabs."

Hub told his phone, "I get the feeling you don't want to talk, but will you listen?" He paused, then added, "Whatever grievance you have, whatever quarrel—surely it doesn't involve these children?"

Frank translated. Still he received no response.

"So I'm gonna ask you," Hub continued, his words measured, "to . . . please . . . let . . . these . . . children go."

Frank translated once more. An eternity seemed to tick by. Just as Frank was concluding that he couldn't get through to the terrorists, the bus doors hissed open.

Six bewildered, ashen-faced children stumbled down the steps to the pavement. The doors hissed shut behind them. Hub and some cops hurried from behind the barricade to help the kids along. Moments later they were safely out of harm's way.

A smattering of applause broke out among the assembled personnel. Frank swallowed hard, amazed that Hub had made this happen. He looked around and glimpsed Elise. Transfixed, blinking, she stared from the car. Frank's amazement expanded a number of degrees. Elise appeared to be holding back tears.

So the woman possessed a human dimension after all. But that didn't mean she had been proved wrong about the terrorists' plans. Frank rallied himself. "Okay," he muttered, "here we go."

"Thank you, sir," Hub was saying to his phone. He kept himself just inside the barricade, within view of the terrorists. "I appreciate that gesture, I really do. The best way to get what you want in these situations is to show yourself to be reasonable. As you've just done." Hub paused so Frank could translate. "Now we've got some more to talk about," Hub continued.

From the car, Elise watched news cameras zoom in for close-ups. She held her breath.

Hub took a few steps toward the bus. "I am unarmed, as you can see," he went on. "So I propose . . ." He took another step forward. "I propose that you let the rest of the passengers go, and I take their place." He gestured in a friendly manner, signaling willingness to be helpful. "That way, there's no pizza deliveries or bathroom breaks to worry about—and all these people"—Hub waved at the SWAT teams—"will disappear." He looked at Frank and waited for the translation.

Frank shook his head gravely, trying to warn Hub that the proposal was a terrible idea. Hub's eyes bored into Frank's, ordering Frank: *Do it.* Translate. Do not let me down now.

Frank translated. Elise gazed at Hub, her face betraying mixed emotions. Like Frank, she thought Hub's plan was nuts. At the same time, though, she had to admire his bravery.

The terrorists didn't reply to Frank's translation. Hub said into his phone, "How about we just start with a few of the elderly people you got on there. It's got to be hard for the older folks to be standing all this time." Hub made eye contact with Frank. Frank translated. He received no response.

But then once again, the bus doors hissed open. A few elderly passengers began to exit, not at all steadily.

Frank sighed with relief. Elise started breathing again.

"Thank you, sir," Hub boomed into his phone. "Now let's just let these—"

A monstrous noise obliterated Hub's voice. The bus dissolved; force rushed from it, lifting Hub into the air and hurling him backward. Hot wind seared him, slapped him with a gale of grit that corroded his skin, his coat, his shoes, and it didn't stop. The blast kept coming and Hub kept flying, back, back through the air as the bus continued to dissolve, erupting into flames now. A cloud of tiny fiery fragments embraced Hub's entire body, reached with sharp fingers into his clothing, his skin, seeming to penetrate even his mind. He hit the pavement and started skidding.

His vision dimmed. The explosion opened a portal; from it a chorus emerged, shrieking a demonic song. The sound became louder, louder, and just when Hub thought it couldn't possibly continue to amplify, it punched through to a new acoustical dimension—unbearably more pure, unbearably more loud—a harmonic fusion that whited out the world.

And still he kept skidding over the pavement.

The shock wave spewed debris across the intersection in all directions. Shrapnel thudded into police cars, bus benches, doorways, into the clothing and flesh of emergency personnel. A grisly mist infused the blast. Salty, hot, with a copper tang, it had pumped through veins instants before; now a reddish film, mixed with shreds of flesh and fragments of bone, it merely discolored the air.

Windows shattered within a five-block radius. Ears rang within a thirty-block radius. Minds came to a sharp point throughout the neighborhood; parents embraced their children. Prayers and curses sounded in thousands of throats.

On the spot where the bus had stood, an oily pyre blazed. Television cameras, aloft and ground-based, recorded every licking flame.

Hub fought to retain consciousness. But in his head the high-pitched noise continued to shrill, deforming his perceptions. He caught sight of someone stooping beside him. Frank, offering help and comfort. Frank's mouth moved; he was talking, loudly from the look of it. But the white-noise shriek obliterated all other sounds.

Hub realized he'd been deafened.

"I'm—all right," he stammered. The words didn't register properly in his head. Hub wondered if he was making any sound at all.

Frank's mouth moved again. Hub focused on the lips, attempting to read them. He realized that Frank was saying, "Just hang in there, buddy."

"Okay," Hub muttered. "Just let me . . ." He shuddered. The white noise wouldn't go away. It seemed to resonate at a subatomic level, canceling out everything else, sealing him into a separate reality from which he would never emerge. Hub gasped for air. Claustrophobia overcame him, followed by nausea. He leaned over and vomited onto the pavement.

Frank clutched his shoulders, trying to steady him.

Hub shook his head. The white noise filled it, but something was striating the outskirts of his mind. A familiar sound. A squealing sound, high-pitched but different, thank God, from the white noise. Hub homed in on it, desperately wanting to reconnect with reality. He wiped his mouth with the sleeve of his coat. The new sound bled through the white noise, louder, louder . . .

Hub realized it was the sound of sirens. A normal sound, of the real world. Not a pleasant sound, given the circumstances that had summoned it. Still, his hearing was coming back.

Frank helped him rise to his feet. Hub asked woozily, "Is anybody . . . ?" He didn't finish the question. But at least he was hearing himself talk.

The look in Frank's eyes hit Hub like a bucket of ice water. He took in what remained of the bus.

A shattered hulk, ragingly on fire.

Hub swayed, feeling dizzy again. The devastation overwhelmed him. Glass, everywhere. Body parts, everywhere. Flames, smoke, an acrid stench. Running cops and firemen and, up in the air, poised like vultures, absorbing everything for their hungry audiences, the TV news choppers. Then Hub caught sight of his car.

Elise Kraft stared from the rear seat. Shrapnel had grazed her face; she was bleeding. Their eyes met. Hub blinked at her.

Elise's gaze held absolute compassion.

9

More than a hundred agents filled the FBI's situation room in the Federal Building. Adrenaline charged the air; the bombing of the #87 bus, and the brutal elegance of its presentation to the press, had replaced business as usual with something akin to a state of war. The masterminds behind the bombing clearly hadn't died on the bus. They'd put together an escalating plan: first the paint attack that had killed no one but drew lots of attention, then a real attack that killed dozens, vaulting the story into the media stratosphere coast-to-coast. These people were serious. No one doubted they would strike again. They had to be stopped.

Compelling though all that was, the single most galvanic force in the room came from Hub. In complete denial of his physical condition, he paced back and forth like a caged animal, issuing a steady flow of orders and inspirational rhetoric. "Every trap, every *hole*," he proclaimed. "I want to rumble every mosque, every community center, every student organization that's ever said an unkind word. I want the heat turned up under all our assets, all our informers, every snitch gets twisted *inside out*. And put some money out on the street. See what falls out of their pockets."

The crowd drank it in, simultaneously awed and concerned. Hub sure as hell knew how to fire up an offensive. Was he physically capable of following through?

Hub turned to Mike Johannson. "Have you got a positive ID on . . ."

"Hub," Mike interrupted. "We don't have positive ID on *anybody*."

Hub nodded, accepting that fact, its implications, for what they were. He declared, "We need more hands." His stare settled on Fred Darius. "Fred—"

"I'm on it," Fred replied instantly. He grabbed a phone and started punching. Rounding up more personnel wouldn't be a problem.

Mike Johannson's comment set off further reverberations in Hub's mind. He realized that no matter how much manpower he put to work, no matter how many leads the extra agents turned up, he was obliged to yank quickly, and hard, on what he already had. So far that consisted of one individual. Hub looked at Tina Osu, and growled, "I want to talk with Khalil."

Tina replied crisply, "He's down the hall." Then, like Fred, she grabbed a phone and stabbed buttons, in search of more bodies to run the case.

Hub knew he was pushing the envelope. He also knew that some of his people were wondering how much of a grip he had. It didn't matter. He had to make things happen.

He launched back into his general spiel to the room. "Conferences with DC at twelve, four, and nine. Call your families, find a sleeping bag, nobody leaves this office until we have a strand to pull. Oklahoma City, people. The first twenty-four hours are the *only* twenty-four hours." His voice lowered; his eyes raked the faces listening to him. "And I don't want to see anybody walking."

Ten minutes later Hub, Tina, and Frank stood outside Khalil's holding cell, watching him on a closed-circuit video monitor. Khalil's face had puffed up; the bruises had darkened into purple welts. Hub studied them with concern. "Doctor seen him?" he asked Tina.

"He's on his way up," Tina replied.

Hub thought a moment. "Got a cigarette?" he inquired.

"You don't smoke," Tina pointed out. A bit puzzled, she dropped her pack into Hub's outstretched hand.

Hub entered the cell. Khalil stared at him nervously. Hub grabbed a chair, turned it backward, and sat quite close to the prisoner.

"Ten thousand dollars," Hub remarked.

Frank translated from the doorway. Khalil feigned ignorance.

"*Khalil,*" Hub snapped. "I want to talk about the *money.*"

Frank rendered Hub's words in Arabic. Khalil maintained his blank expression.

"Okay," Hub murmured. He reached in a pocket and casually extracted the cigarette pack. Khalil's eyes widened. Frank looked at the small scars that cratered the man's neck. In how many holding cells and other unpleasant places had Khalil been subjected to the business end of a lit cigarette?

Hub smiled at the man, not reassuringly. Despite Khalil's dark complexion and darker bruises, he visibly paled. Under ordinary circumstances Hub was capable of looking fairly scary. In the aftermath of the #87 bus's destruction—his close-cropped hair speckled with residues of dried blood and crushed glass—he looked downright terrifying. Hub's mood also contributed. The sight of a busload of people turning to mist had not brought out his sentimental side.

He struck a match. The rasping sound had an effect on Khalil: His forehead beaded with sweat. Hub brought the flame to the cigarette and inhaled deeply, taking his time. The cigarette's tip ignited. Hub inhaled again; the tip glowed a bright orange-red. Involuntarily, Khalil recoiled in his chair. Hub turned to Frank, and remarked, "He doesn't like secondhand smoke."

Frank nodded. Hub turned back to Khalil, gesturing casually with the cigarette. "You ready to talk about money?" he asked quietly.

Frank was about to translate. But a switch inside Khalil had just flipped; he suddenly was willing to play ball. He started speed-rapping in Arabic.

"He says he loves America," Frank translated. "He only wanted to get away from the security forces at home."

Khalil's volubility didn't slow. Tears welled in his eyes, streamed down his discolored face. Frank kept up with him. "He says he's sorry, but he didn't know he was doing something bad." Khalil slipped from his chair and knelt at Hub's feet, his hands clasped in the classic stance of one pleading for mercy. "His cousin introduced him," Frank went on, "to a man who promised him two hundred dollars for his dowry if he'd bring the suitcase to an address in Brooklyn." Frank glanced at Hub. "He's a cutout."

Hub asked questions until Khalil had revealed what little he knew.

Outside the holding cell a few minutes later, Hub returned the cigarette pack to Tina. "Nasty habit," remarked. Then he added more sharply, "Thirty-eight thirty Flatbush Avenue."

The SWAT team pulled up to 3830 Flatbush Avenue in an unmarked van. Agents spilled out, rifles at the ready, their torsos thick with armored vests. They entered the building and located the apartment.

Its door gave way under a series of well-placed kicks. Agents swarmed in. An empty apartment awaited them. There was nothing there of interest except for one item.

On the floor, a fax machine was generating reams of printout. Each page bore repeats of the same two-word message:

RELEASE HIM.

In addition to confirming that the terrorists' game plan involved the release of an unknown individual, the raid yielded one other fact. The rental arrangement for the apartment at 3830 Flatbush hadn't left much of a paper trail. No checks or money orders had been used to take possession. The tenants had transacted the rental strictly in cash.

Hub wasted no time putting the information to use. He convened another meeting in the Federal Building situation room. "We want every rental agreement from every landlord in Brooklyn," he told the assembled agents. "Hotels, motels, flophouses." The agents pondered the assignment's logistics. Brooklyn held a very large number of rental housing units. In fact, if considered on its own apart from the rest of New York City, the borough ranked as America's third-largest city after Chicago and Los Angeles. Even a full-court press using the combined resources of the Bureau and the NYPD would have trouble nailing down the particulars of every last tenant-landlord relationship.

Mindful of that reality, Hub supplied a way to streamline the search. "It's cash, guys. They're the only ones in America using cash."

An hour later, a technician dimmed the situation room's lights and turned on an overhead projector. He inserted a transparency. An image came onscreen that resembled a simplified seismographic chart; lines spiked and dipped at varying levels. "This is a spectrograph of the Semtex used in the bomb," the technician explained, referring to the Czech-made plastic explosive that terrorists prized for its high yield, moldable malleability, and, unless ignited, chemical inertness. "Look at the benzene spike," the technician went on, indicating a peak. "This is the genuine article."

He inserted another transparency. "Now . . ." The technician paused, giving his audience time to register the fact that the new image looked to be an exact reproduction of the first. "This one's from the barracks in Dhahran." He referred to the massive explosion that had taken down the Khobar Towers building in Saudi Arabia. "As you can see, the signature is identical."

Hub recalled what Elise had said about the men who'd seized the #87 bus. *They're the real deal.*

Another hour went by. Hub dropped by the workstation of a computer specialist named Bob Whitney, who was cross-referencing data from previous attacks. Whitney's screen displayed digitized photographs of various suspected terrorists. He scrolled past an image of a sheik named Ahmed bin Talal. An image of the gutted barracks came up.

Hub wanted to know if anyone in this particular rogue's gallery had ever struck with the *modus operandi* used earlier that day. "Can you ask it if they've ever hit buses?"

Whitney nodded, and typed in commands. A series of images scrolled down, featuring buses that had met violent ends. They were labeled with place names: Tel Aviv, Jerusalem, Beirut. Whitney instructed the computer to compare each case with the Brooklyn bus. None was a match. "Not according to the mainframe," Whitney reported.

Hub frowned. There had to be a reason the barracks bombers had selected a target that they didn't seem to have gone after before. Why the switch? What might it have to do with the demand for a mystery man's release?

Were the bombers sending a message in their choice of explosive, choice of target? If so, what was that message?

Hub drove out to the bomb scene with Frank Haddad and Danny Sussman. He'd established a dozen communication links with the site and been getting steady reports every twenty minutes. But he needed to know how things were going through his own two eyes, his own two ears. Moreover, he wanted to confirm that his technical people were cranking themselves to the max.

The site now resembled an archeological dig. Custom floodlamps on stanchions rendered the daylight unnaturally bright. Forensic experts on their hands and knees were examining the bus's shattered hulk, using black lights and delicately brushed-on chemicals to search for latent prints. Varicolored string divided the site into grids; every millimeter that hadn't already been eyeballed and probed soon would be.

Frank and Danny watched Hub make rounds, pausing to speak with every supervisor one by one. "With a Q-Tip," they overheard him instruct a fellow in a white coat. "Bone shards, hair, *fingernails . . .*"

Although Hub wasn't telling the man anything new, he was sharing his sense of urgency. If he could inspire an extra iota of dedication, one more increment of concentration—that might make all the difference.

Danny saw a different picture. Hub's intensity struck him as counterproductive: more nerve-wracking than inspiring. He muttered to Frank, "He's way over his head."

Frank snapped, "Shut the fuck up and go give somebody a parking ticket." No one made cracks like that about his boss. Especially not an NYPD liaison who didn't know shit about the FBI's ability to push through limits.

Hub checked in on Stan Weir, the forensics lab's fingerprint expert. Weir was methodically going through the contents of a plastic bag. Gamy contents, thoroughly unappealing in appearance, texture, odor: They consisted of severed fingertips and loose teeth.

Weir used a modified computer scanner to lift prints from the fingertips and digitize them. The scanner also was able to digitize subtle 3-D characteristics of the teeth. A mainframe computer meanwhile ran searches of several different international databases that contained the fingerprints and dental records of suspected terrorists.

"Any matches?" Hub asked.

"Not yet," Weir replied. He didn't look up from his work.

Hub made more rounds, offering encouragement, keeping his people on their toes. At one point in the early afternoon he passed through the situation room.

A wall held a bank of video monitors. They were tuned to different networks, cable and broadcast. All of them had suspended regular programming to carry the bus-bombing story.

The network news chiefs directing coverage of the tragedy had achieved a rare unanimity. Every last screen was replaying the explosion, over and over.

Hub listened to snippet of audio: "Today, Tel Aviv has come to Brooklyn. The question is— why?"

You got it, Hub thought hollowly.

The images had been shot from different angles, with different degrees of close-up. But they all contained the same core elements. The bus, standing alone in the middle of the Brooklyn intersection. The passengers massed in the aisle, shadowy figures among them. The bus's doors swinging open. The elderly passengers tottering out, their faces contorted with fear. And then, the explosion. Some of the news directors were rolling that part in slow motion. Hub watched the bus vibrate, then gradually fragment. He watched the exiting passengers take lazy airborne trajectories. The windows blew out; debris ejected in jerky cascades. Then, fearsomely spastic, the fireball expanded.

Some of the images included a well-built African-American man wearing a long dark overcoat. He stood outside the bus, a cell phone to his head. When the bus blew he, too, was sent flying through the air.

Hub didn't care about his presence in the scene. He'd survived, after all. But the passengers were a different story. Suddenly he couldn't take it anymore, the mindlessly repeating images of death, the idea that just about everyone with a TV set could watch this, was watching this, everywhere in the world. His eyes stung. He had to turn away; people in the situation room might get the wrong impression.

Bob Whitney, the computer specialist, glimpsed the expression on Hub's face. "You okay?" he asked.

Hub didn't know how to reply. But he didn't have to reply; Stan Weir had burst into the room. Hub's pulse quickened.

"Got one!" Weir exclaimed.

10

Hub stood with Tina Osu on the situation room's raised dais. Twenty agents were fanned out before them.

"Ladies and gentlemen," Hub said, "meet the late Ali Waziri." He projected a photo of the man in question on the screen on the wall. "Tina talked to the Israelis and traced this sucker to a group operating out of Ramallah. That's the West Bank, not the West Side—for those of you just joining us from Nebraska."

Chuckles greeted the comment. Hub had delivered just the right touch of levity; tension eased. After an exhausting bitch of a day, one filled with a thousand dead ends, mounting pressure, and Hub's indefatigable example of how to squeeze the case harder, then even harder, his core team was hearing the first good news.

Tina took over the briefing. She said with her customary cool, "Okay, we've pulled his landing card and his I-94. So now we know he came in three days ago, out of Frankfurt."

She pointed at the bank of monitors. They were off; no one needed to see yet another replay of the bus's evaporation. Tina was directing the agents' attention to a linear display of differently colored pieces of paper below the monitors. The first segment recorded Ali Waziri's arrival in New York. The final segment noted his seizure of, then death aboard, the bus. The segments in between were blank.

"What we need now," Tina went on, "is to fill in the time between his arrival and the incident. All known associations, and most of all, we need an address."

The meeting broke up. Finally, the Task Force had something concrete to go on.

The time-line display under the monitors acquired more detail. Slowly but surely, Ali Waziri's movements were beginning to come into focus.

The effort required the collection, collation, and sifting of a vast amount of data. Phone technicians worked continuously on adding tie-lines, dedicated fax lines, WATS lines, scrambled lines. Lack of time prevented concealment of the auxiliary equipment. The result: a spectacle of technology gone amok. Cables snaked everywhere in a steady metastasis around the room.

Danny Sussman and Frank Haddad had teamed up to glean whatever they could from Ali Waziri's documentation. They pored over the I-94 entrance visa form that Tina Osu had mentioned. Arcane INS codes filled the form's boxes. "IAP66," Frank read aloud. "What's IAP66?"

Danny flipped through an INS manual. "Hold on, hold on, I'm looking it up—"

"Today, Danny," Frank said impatiently.

Hub paced back and forth nearby, listening to the interchange. His presence did nothing to diminish the ongoing friction in Frank and Danny's working relationship.

"Wait, wait," Danny said feverishly. "Here we go," he added, a finger pinpointing a paragraph of explanatory text. "Student visa, J-1."

Hub froze, then wheeled to the two men. "Where's the original?" he asked.

"In his passport," Danny replied.

"Which is . . ." Frank said. He grimaced, considering the passport's present state. "Vaporized."

Hub demanded, "Where's the copy?" There had to be a copy, or more likely several. One of government's most ironclad rules required the multiplication of paper.

"At the point of issuance," Frank said. "Could be the American Consulate in Tel Aviv. The American

Consulate in Amman, Cairo, Alexandria, Riyadh—all an easy drive from the West Bank."

Geography whirled in Hub's mind, along with the filing cabinets of distant State Department offices. He wondered how long it would take to get those offices in gear . . . suddenly he felt a little unsteady. The situation room seemed to rotate around him; a rush of nausea soured his stomach. "What time is it?" he muttered.

Danny checked his watch. "Three-fifteen," he replied, "P.M."

Hub didn't appear to register the information.

"When's the last time you ate?" Danny inquired.

Hub shook his head. The last time he ate? He had no idea. Fred Darius approached, his boyish face on point. *Good*, thought Hub. *Fred's got something*. Maybe it would distract him from the mysterious disfunction in his gut. . . .

"Sir," Fred said urgently, "they want you in the lab."

Frank and Fred accompanied Hub to the forensics lab. In it Stan Weir was examining something through the lab's heaviest-duty electron microscope. "Take a look," Weir said to Hub, standing aside.

Hub peered through the 'scope. It was trained on a long, thin strandlike object. Fiber of some kind. Weir said, "Pure, unadulterated Egyptian cotton."

Fred jumped to what seemed like the evident conclusion. "You're saying they're Egyptian?" he asked.

"No," replied Weir. "*No*," he added with more emphasis, "I'm just saying . . ."

Hub realized where Weir was going. "It's what they use for funerals," he said. "The guy was wearing a shroud."

Frank and Hub exchanged loaded glances. The terrorists had apparently planned their own deaths with ritualistic care. That heightened the threat their controllers posed. Politics didn't motivate these people; holiness did. They saw themselves as martyrs who would receive just rewards in the kingdom of Allah. Rationality, accordingly, wasn't a factor. They just didn't care if they died. On the contrary—in their minds, death would bring them the greatest imaginable glory.

In other words, they were capable of anything.

Frank and Hub shared a wordless realization. Elise had been right. The planners of the #87 bus bombing weren't amateurs. They most definitely were the real deal.

Hub said to Frank, "Let's see if she's ready to talk."

Elise sat quietly in her holding cell, with the stillness of one who has been there before. Hub entered. She greeted him with an unruffled stare.

Hub said, "I thought one phone call and you were out of here."

"Didn't make the call," Elise replied.

"Why not?" Hub asked. It wasn't the first time Elise had demonstrated her determination to keep a low profile. This didn't make Hub any less wary. What the hell did Elise have to hide?

As usual she declined to explain herself. Her neutral gaze gave away nothing. "Are you all right?" she asked. No load in the question. An inquiry, nothing more.

Hub cocked his head. "Just some tinnitus in my left ear," he said casually.

"That's not what I mean," Elise said.

"I'm fine," Hub replied, meeting her stare.

For a number of seconds they regarded each other across the professional chasm stretching between them. Silence deepened. It didn't bother Elise.

Finally, Hub said, "I need to know what I don't know."

Elise smiled faintly. "Life's too short.

But something had shifted in Elise's tone. Her flippancy notwithstanding, she seemed to have opened up a crack. "You hungry?" Hub asked.

Elise's eyebrows rose. "We ordering in?"

Hub contemplated eating Chinese takeout in Elise's cell. Then he decided it was time to try a different tack.

* * *

Twenty minutes later they were sitting at the counter of a downtown delicatessen. Elise sipped tea. Corned beef sandwiches were on the way.

Their conversation centered on the strand of Egyptian cotton that the forensics lab had found. "The funeral shroud is the final step in the ritual of self-purification," Elise explained. "First a fast, then—"

"Then the washing of the body," Hub interrupted. "Then the shroud. I saw it on *60 Minutes*. Tell me something I don't know."

Elise pursed her lips. Though her eyes remained expressionless, Hub sensed that cogs were revolving in her mind, performing a routine evaluation: How much to reveal? And when?

She exhaled, and said, "Last March in Iraq we identified the man we believe responsible for the bombing of the barracks in Dhahran. In August, he went to Lebanon. Where he was . . ." She paused, looking for the right word; or, more likely, reluctant to say it. "Extracted."

"Extracted?" Hub asked. Alarms buzzed in the back of his mind. "Extracted by whom?"

Elise's face remained opaque. A reminder that there were places she would not, could not, go.

"I see," Hub said.

"His name is Sheik Ahmed bin Talal," Elise went on. "He's Iraqi. And something of a religious leader."

"With something of a devoted following?" Hub inquired.

Elise nodded. The simple gesture spoke volumes: "The real deal."

The sandwiches arrived. Elise took a hefty bite.

"Okay," Hub said, his manner reasonable, striving to reach out, make a concession, find common ground. "I can understand why we might not want to publicize the fact that our government's in the kidnapping business—but why not tell us?"

"He's still being . . ." Elise paused, again demonstrating hesitancy about choice of words. "Debriefed." Hub pondered the choice. "They're not ready to go public with charges," Elise added.

"What else you got on his followers?" Hub asked.

"Clearly, they're committed."

"Meaning?" Hub pressed.

"In this game," Elise replied, "the most committed wins."

"So they'll just keep coming until we release him," Hub said uneasily.

"Unless," Elise rejoined, "we match their commitment with our own."

Hub thought a moment. "What about talking to this sheik?"

Elise shook her head. "You don't think they've got guys talking to the sheik? Except the sheik isn't talking."

"So who's giving orders?" Hub demanded. "How do they coordinate, pick their targets?"

"Believe me," Elise declared, "we've put every resource we've got onto that very question." She set down her fork. "Otherwise . . ." Her voice trailed off. "We wait."

"We wait," Hub echoed glumly.

Elise looked into Hub's eyes. She said with quiet empathy, "If there's anybody on Earth who knows how you feel, it's me." Elise's mask had slipped; suddenly she seemed to be speaking from her heart. The idea unnerved Hub. The likes of Elise, speaking from the heart? "But you've got to let it go," she continued. "Those people were dead the minute they got on the bus."

Not a cheering image, Hub reflected. But dead-on accurate. It raised a couple of questions that had been haunting him. How many more buses were doomed? How many people would board them?

Frank Haddad materialized at the counter. "Sorry, boss," he said, apologizing for the intrusion. "Hello, Elise." Frank's eyes alighted on what remained of Elise's sandwich. "Mmmmmm—is that pastrami?" He helped himself to a slice. His mouth full, he added, "Oh, yeah. We made the guy in the picture."

Hub, Frank, and Elise drove in Hub's car to a Brooklyn café that catered to the local Arab intelligentsia. Three backup agents followed in another car.

Hub paused in the café's entrance to survey the scene. Raucous Arabic streamed from people crowded around small tables, mostly young men. Cigarette smoke—pungent, richer than the standard American brands—streamed from them as well. Every last patron seemed to be smoking.

"My people," Frank remarked with a rueful stare. "The last of the unambivalent smokers." He shook his head. "Monsters," he added softly. "The toughest motherfucker in Bed-Stuy is a muffin compared to some of these guys."

Hub caught sight of the good-looking Palestinian with whom Khalil had chatted early that morning—the chat that Khalil aborted when his West Bank sixth sense alerted him to the FBI surveillance operation. The fellow unquestionably was the same guy. His face matched the one that the FBI had captured via telephoto lens. He looked to be ready to take his leave. Hub, Frank, and Elise watched him call for his bill.

"His name is Samir Nazhde," Frank told the others. "Teaches Arab Studies at Brooklyn College. He sponsored Ali Waziri's student visa." Hub's eyebrows tightened as he mentally filed that fact. "And dig this," Frank went on. "His brother blew up a movie theater in Tel Aviv."

Elise cleared her throat. "You might consider

leaving him alone," she said casually. Too casually.

Hub turned to her, all ears. "Why would I consider doing that?" he asked.

Elise stared at Samir Nazhde. He was counting out cash on his table. "Play him like a cop," Elise said, disapproval tingeing her voice, "and haul him in and get your arrest." She shrugged. "Or tag him and let him lead you to the really big fish."

Frank cursed in Arabic under his breath. "You're fishing," he said scornfully. "And he's getting visas for bombers."

"You ever hear of catch and release?" Elise asked him.

"Yes, and he's on the next plane to Tunis," Frank shot back.

Samir made his way to the exit. Hub gave Elise a pensive look. A snap judgment awaited, one he wasn't prepared to let Elise make. "Take him down," he said.

Frank keyed his radio. "Go," he told it.

Hub strode back to the car. Frank and Elise followed as the three backup agents braced Samir, politely but firmly. Samir realized right away that resistance wasn't an option. The agents led him to Hub's car. He slid onto the backseat next to Elise.

Hub watched in the rearview mirror. Elise and Nazhde exchanged fleeting glances. A spark seemed to pass between them. Veiled recognition? Acknowledgment?

Hub wondered if he'd started imagining things that didn't exist. He reminded himself that with Elise, what did or did not exist remained very much an open question.

11

Frank leaned over the car's front seat. "Samir Nazhde," he said to the detainee, "my name is Frank Haddad. I'm a federal agent. We have reason to believe you are an accessory to the bombing of Bus 87."

Samir's eyes blazed incredulity. "Are you *crazy*?" he exclaimed.

"You are an associate of Ali Waziri," Frank declared, his voice taut with accusation.

"*Who?*" Samir demanded. "I know no one by that name."

Elise stared at the mid-distance beyond her window, detaching herself from the interchange. Or pretending to, Hub thought as he watched in the rearview mirror.

"You got him a student visa," Frank pointed out.

Samir blinked. He said, "I sign these applications as a matter of course, hundreds of them." He shrugged philosophically. "Everyone wants to come to the land of opportunity and *Baywatch*."

Hub watched Elise suppress a smile.

"You spent two years in Israeli jails during the Intifada," Frank went on.

Samir's eyes narrowed. "The only ones who didn't," he replied, "were women like you."

Frank's arm lashed out, backhanding Samir across the mouth. Samir shook his head, fury glazing his face. He spat out imprecations in Arabic. Frank responded in kind.

"Frank," Hub said quietly but with commanding force.

"Sorry," Frank told his boss. "Family matter." To Samir he said, "You're going downtown, my friend."

"You cannot hold me," Samir protested. "I know my rights. I watch American television!"

Frank said, "Defrauding the INS is a federal offense." He gestured at the waiting agents. "Reservation for one, please."

The agents hauled Samir out of the car.

Later, shortly after midnight, Hub, Frank, and Elise entered the FBI situation room. The cubicles formed a random checkerboard of light and dark. Some agents were still working, others had fallen asleep at their desks, still others had sacked out in sleeping bags along the walls.

"Club Fed," Elise commented.

Danny Sussman was draped across his desk, facedown. Frank leaned over him; he sang in a deceptively sweet brogue, "Oh Danny-boy, the perps, the perps are call-ing . . ."

Danny twitched, then woke, his face bleary with sleep.

Frank informed him vigorously, "We need a search warrant on Samir."

"Frank," Hub called. "C'mere a sec. I want to show you something." He led Frank into another cubicle. Elise, perched on a nearby desk, was using a phone. She paused to watch Hub and Frank.

Hub said with restrained intensity, "Frank, you ever hit a prisoner again, I'll have your badge."

Frank gulped for air, his color rising. "Someday," he said heatedly, "I will tell you what those people did to my village in '71."

Hub looked at Frank, hoping he would cool off. In a gesture of conciliation, he touched Frank's arm. "Okay," Hub said. "But right now, act as if I'm capable of saying something *funny*." Thinly, he smiled. Frank chaired the Task Force's wisecrack department. Maybe he'd get a grip on professional standards of conduct if, for just a moment, he saw Hub as the resident jokester. "Now," Hub said soothingly, "let's go see about that warrant."

Frank nodded. He had to nod. The ASAC had spoken.

They left the cubicle. Elise followed. As they passed Sussman, Hub told him, "Find me a judge who'll play ball this time. And set up a polygraph for Samir."

"I still don't understand why we're tipping our hand with him," Elise complained.

"What's there to tip?" Frank asked.

Hub wheeled to Elise. "You're just trying to protect your asset," he declared.

For an instant, Elise looked startled. She swiftly recovered.

"Aren't you, Elise?" Hub demanded. "He's your Joe, your *asset*. He's *working* for you, you're his case officer—*right?*"

Elise weighed her response. Frank watched her closely. Hub, he concluded, had cut through to the sinew here.

"Sometimes," Elise said carefully, "in addition to being a nationality, being a Palestinian is also a . . ." She sighed, unsure how to euphemize what she had in mind. "A profession," she said. "A lucrative one."

Hub's stare didn't waver. "Meaning," he said, repeating himself and driving home the point, "he's your Joe."

"Mine," Elise said, her eyes engaging Hub's stare. "Yours. The Israelis'. The Saudis'." An edge crept into her voice as she added, "At one time or another, everybody in the Middle East has slept with everybody else."

"So you're saying you sleep around?" Frank said suggestively.

"Only professionally," Elise replied, not missing a beat.

"So we share him," Hub proposed.

"No," Elise replied, her tone categorical.

She was testing the limits, seeing how far she could push things. Hub wasn't shy about pushing back. He turned to Frank and snapped, "Call INS. Find out his status and start deportation proceedings."

"I can't let you do that," Elise said quickly.

"Oh, you can't let me do that," Hub echoed, his voice thick with sarcasm. "What *precisely* is your involvement with these people?"

Elise sighed again. She crossed her arms, then uncrossed them, and said tentatively, "Samir's been a very important . . ." She stopped, again in need of a euphemism. She found it: "A very important project of mine. For some time, too. I'm the only one he'll deal with. He's very well connected. And," she concluded meaningfully—as if pointing out something that Hub would do well to keep in mind— "extremely high-strung."

Hub considered what she'd said. It didn't pass muster. It didn't even come close, no matter how high-strung Samir Nadzhe might happen to be. In fact, Hub approved of that attribute in a source. It encouraged the spilling of guts. He told Frank, "Call the judge."

Elise also turned to Frank. Challenge in her voice, her manner that of one professional testing the expertise of another, she asked, "How easy is it to get inside, Frank?" The question hit a nerve; Frank's mouth tightened. "How good are your sources in Jihad?" Elise demanded. "How many people you got in Hamas?"

Frank shook his head. He couldn't contest the case Elise was making. She was on target, he knew only too well.

Hub absorbed Frank's reaction. Elise meanwhile clocked Hub. A subtle dynamic passed between them; in different ways, all three were forced to acknowledge realities they couldn't avoid.

"No surveillance," Elise said, putting cards on the table. "I've seen your deft touch."

The gibe referred to the botched tailing of Khalil on Atlantic Avenue that morning. It didn't faze Hub. "Daily reports," he said tersely. "We tap his phone."

"And I get to see the transcripts," Elise said, shoring up her flanks.

"Fair enough," Hub said.

"And I run him," Elise said, reaching for position.

"*We* share him," Hub said, heading her off.

"Done," Elise said with finality.

Hub told Frank, "Let him fly." He turned back to Elise, and warned, "But we better start seeing product."

Elise nodded. At least for the moment, the horse trades satisfied both sides.

Hub wasn't quite finished. "Any more surprises for me?" he asked Elise.

"Not tonight," Elise replied impassively.

"Then I'm going home to get some things," Hub announced. He looked bone tired.

"I'll have somebody drive you," Frank said.

Hub shook his head. "I'll grab a cab." He strode off.

Frank looked his new partner up and down. "Elise," he said, echoing the meaningful tone she'd used a minute before, "I'm really high-strung, too."

Elise gave him a serene smile. Then she walked away.

Frank stared after her. He knew the truth of the comment she'd made about every power in the Middle East at one point or another getting in bed. And he understood her tacit admission that she herself had slept around. It was the way things played out in the labyrinth of factions that defined that part of the world. Often, it was the only way one stood a chance of *becoming* a player.

Those were the facts, pure and simple. That

Elise knew them added to her credentials; it expanded the possibility she might be useful. But it also raised a problem. If Frank and Hub got in bed with Elise, who else might crawl in and join them?

Something about Elise made Frank feel unclean. Hub, he knew, felt the same way. But Hub had done the right thing.

Without Elise's cooperation, they easily might end up groping thin air.

Hub stood on the corner outside the Federal Building, scanning Broadway for a taxi. Not much pedestrian traffic at 1:03 A.M. this part of downtown. Not a whole lot of action in the streets, either.

But a cab approached, its on-duty signals lit. Hub flagged it down. The cab slowed. A face stared through the windshield; the driver, checking Hub out. When he saw a black man standing in the darkness he gunned the car and sped off.

A red light stopped him at the end of the block. Hub sprinted to the cab. Just as the light was about to change he slapped his badge on the windshield. The driver stared at it. He nodded, experiencing a sudden attitude adjustment.

Hub climbed in and gave his apartment's address. The cab hurtled uptown through Manhattan's dark canyons. Streetlights strobed the car's interior, washing over the front seat, the bullet-resistant partition, the driver's framed ID certificate. Hub glimpsed the name: Abdul Hassam.

Exhaustedly, he shook his head.

A few minutes later Hub stood under the hot spray of his shower. He ran his hands through his hair, dislodging tiny chunks of shattered glass. Dried blood dissolved under his fingertips, darkening the rivulets flowing from his head, his hands, putting a dense sepia color in the water circling the drain. Whose blood was this? Not his.

Maybe it had filled the veins of the elderly folks who mistakenly thought they were going free while stumbling off the bus. Or maybe it had pounded to the heartbeats of the men who just then decided to pull their detcords, say good-bye, and ride Semtex to Allah. Most likely, of course, it was a mixture. A miscegenation born of hate.

Not that it made any difference whose remains were circling the drain. Lives had been lost in a manner that promised more death; there lay the significance of Hub's tinted water. He slumped against the shower's wall and closed his eyes.

The open palm cracked across Elise's face.

She recoiled. Samir loomed over her, his face contorted with rage. "You let him *hit me!*" he snarled.

Moments before Elise had admitted him to her dimly lit apartment. Pain flamed through her head.

Not for the first time, she wondered if Samir was really worth it.

He bellowed, "You cannot care about me and let such things *happen!*"

"Next time don't be such a smart-ass," Elise muttered.

Contempt ignited in Samir's eyes, denaturing his handsome looks. "Sometimes," he said viciously, "I hate you because you are so American. It makes me want to hurt you." He grimaced, showing his white teeth. "I think about fucking you and hurting you."

Elise tasted brine in her mouth. She resisted an urge to spit the blood in Samir's face. Long before, she'd struck a fateful bargain. This was part of its ongoing price. "You want to fuck me?" she asked dispassionately, getting down to business. He did want to fuck her, of course. He always did; it helped him control his emotions. But first he would have to fulfill his end of the deal. "Tell me about the visas," she said.

"I don't need to tell you anything," Samir said with loathing.

To a considerable degree it was self-loathing, Elise long since had learned. "No?" she said, her voice quietly ominous. "Do we really need to have this conversation again?"

Samir heard the threat in her tone. His stare wavered; he lowered his eyes.

As always, Elise took advantage of the opening. She stroked Samir's arm. Endearingly, she said, "I need you to help me." Samir's eyelashes fluttered. "I need you to be strong," she continued, zeroing in on his weak point without a trace of irony. "As you have always been strong. For *both* of us." Samir licked his lips. "Samir?" Elise whispered. "Look at me. . . ."

Hub's beeper went off. He woke with a start, registering darkness. A pile of documents covered his lap. Visa applications, he groggily remembered. He realized he was sitting in his living-room armchair.

He set aside the applications. Then he rose, stretched, and quickly got dressed.

Samir pushed Elise onto the bed. She didn't resist as he clambered on, then roughly flipped her face-down. It was part of the game. One of the dirtier aspects of her carefully honed strategy to stay in control.

The passivity encouraged Samir's delusion that he was in control. Elise barely shuddered. She could take it. Samir wasn't really fucking her, nor was he really hurting her, for in his mind he was doing those things to the United States of America—acts that replenished him only to make him Elise's creature more than ever. Had Elise not been able to maintain that odd loop of logic, she would have succumbed to the pain. But she was able, and didn't.

Part of the price. Part of the gain.

Samir grunted as he finished. Victorious, he kissed the nape of her neck. Elise sighed. Her eyes, not present, held the thousand-yard stare.

When Hub left his apartment building Frank was waiting with a Styrofoam cup. Hub sipped the hot coffee. He didn't have to thank Frank for the gesture. Body language sufficed. The semiceremonial way Frank handed the cup over, the semiseignorial way Hub accepted it. Styrofoam in the building's entryway had become a ritual between them.

Elise lay in bed while Samir smoked beside her. "Some people just cannot live in the camps," he said reflectively. "For my brother, it was already like dying. The only thing he lived for was movies."

She watched him stub out the cigarette, then sit up and reach for a fresh one. Nicotine helped Samir. It both enlivened him and calmed him down.

"And then some sheik tells him that to die for Allah is beautiful," he went on. "If he does this thing, our parents will be taken care of, and he will live on in paradise with seventy virgins." His eyes danced at the idea. "Seventy."

Elise knew of sheiks who promised seven hundred.

Samir exhaled pungent smoke. "And my brother, he needs to believe it very much, so he straps ten sticks of dynamite to his chest and goes to the movies." He laughed; more with chagrin than mirth. "And I become a VIP. It is very confusing."

"So who are you afraid of betraying?" Elise asked, picking up a thread of the conversation they'd abandoned a few minutes before. "You know these people. They bomb, they maim. Do they represent the Palestine you want to build?" She glanced at him, her eyes oblique. "They're using you."

"You are using me, too!" Samir blurted, exhaling storm clouds of smoke. "Everybody uses the Palestinians! We are the whores of the Middle East!"

A distinction not confined to Palestine, Elise reflected. She didn't give voice to the thought. Samir sometimes seemed to revel in his whoredom. It helped him feel sorry for himself.

He glared at her, his animosity coming back. "You make reports about our little talks?" he asked scathingly. "What about fucking me?"

"I had to get special permission for that," Elise replied, her tone suggestive. Samir's glare dimmed a bit. Such remarks reinforced an impression had generated from the beginning of their relationship: of an invisible pyramid of power, upside down, with the point hovering over their heads, that kept track of their every move. Even the sex. Especially the sex.

Unnerved, Samir got up and crossed the room. He stood naked before the uncurtained window, scanning the night. Wondering if it was scanning him back.

The night was, in fact, doing just that. Hub stood on a rooftop across the way, his long dark coat merging with shadow, a pair of 10x50 binoculars pressed to his eyes. The window framed Samir nicely. It gave him the look of an outsize nude in a portrait gallery.

Frank stood beside Hub, also lost in shadow. "Beats cable," he cracked.

12

The next day Hub and Frank launched the Elise Kraft surveillance in earnest. It didn't unfold with the seat-of-the-pants improvisation that had compromised the surveillance of Khalil. The two dozen agents involved kept a careful distance from Elise and Samir. Listening devices and 600mm lenses bridged the gap.

Although neither Elise nor Samir seemed to feel the heat, Hub's people tracked and recorded their every activity, including the most incidental. Cameras clicked far beyond Elise's earshot as she set off on her morning jog. Cameras clicked as she blow-dried her hair; wiretaps picked up conversations from the phones she used. So it went with Samir. Cameras and listening devices documented his chats with students, his meetings with colleagues in the Arab Studies Department at Brooklyn College, his lunch break, his afternoon on-campus rounds.

At noon Elise bought a hot dog from a street vendor. Moments after she'd left the cart, agents seized it and detained the flabbergasted vendor. He wasn't released until Hub's people had determined that he hadn't served, knowingly or unknowingly, as a dead drop for passing messages.

Hub wanted to read the two lives forward and backward, up and down, inside and out. He wanted their deepest patterns. Elise's pledge to cooperate just wasn't good enough. Deception ruled her profession in ways she might not be able to control. And while Hub had to give her credit for essentially admitting as much—"Any more surprises for me?" "Not tonight."—he couldn't risk the possibility that she was playing a more devious game than even her Langley superiors knew. Elise could be entangling him in a scheme the outer limits of which hadn't yet begun to appear.

How far was she prepared to go in the name of "commitment"? The more Hub thought about it, the more significant Elise's invocation of the concept seemed. Her use of Samir suggested that commitment took her pretty damn far; she manipulated him with sex, a sadomasochistic psychological relationship, and God knew what else. Hub refused to take unnecessary chances.

Bottom line, he refused to be used.

He'd decided to run the inquiry from his apartment rather than the office, to try to forestall moles. With twelve hundred agents and eight hundred support personnel spread through seven full floors of the Federal Building, he couldn't be sure that spies weren't in place, especially if Elise had Agency backup, and perhaps other kinds of backup as well. Of course, Elise might have tapped resources that could compromise Hub's apartment—scarcely a harder target than the office. But he needed to stay organized somewhere. Home was the best he could do.

In truth, his apartment seemed more a home, not less of one, with the office transplanted to it. His usual activities there consisted of little beyond sleep and showers. That had changed. For the first time, he felt as if he actually lived there.

By midmorning results started to flood in. Reams of surveillance photos covered the sofa, coffee table, and chairs, along with transcripts of interviews and wiretaps. Samir's bank and credit-card records alone filled several cardboard boxes.

Hub sorted through it all, getting a general picture. Nothing special leapt out. The deep patterns, if they existed, had so far eluded his reach.

At dusk he and Frank were sitting in a car outside a Brooklyn mosque. They knew from an intercepted phone call that Elise planned to attend evening services. She appeared right on schedule, a spring in her step, smartly dressed. Before entering, observant of custom, she settled a veil over her head.

Then she went directly to the women's gallery. A *mullah* was addressing the faithful from the *minbar*, the Islamic equivalent of a pulpit. His topic concerned the bus bombing. "Where in the Koran," he asked with somber indignation, "does it teach us to kill and maim in such cowardly ways? These people are an abomination who compound their sins—"

Hub and Frank listened to the address from a speaker in their car: "—by using the name of Allah *in vain?*"

Frank agreed with the *mullah's* sentiments, to the point that hearing them felt almost like physical relief. But Hub, he noticed, was grimacing, and swallowing, with a degree of trouble. He didn't look well. "You all right?" Frank asked.

Hub gestured at his left ear. The tinnitus, Frank realized. Residual damage from the bus bombing.

The ASAC didn't want to talk about it. "We've been up their butts with a microscope and come up with bupkiss," he grumbled. "I figure we've violated the First, Fourth, and Fifth Amendments, and it's not even dinnertime. I'm *peachy*."

Frank nodded. It was a good thing that Hub didn't serve with the constabularies of Ramallah or Haifa. There, few people thought twice about cutting corners with rights. Discomfiture with the issue was viewed as quaint at best.

*   *   *

That night Hub returned to the rooftop across from the windows of Elise's apartment.

Elise occupied an armchair well within, reading a book. A tame evening for a spook, Hub thought bemusedly, with a measure of suspicion. Home alone with a book?

Time passed. Not even the phone disturbed the apartment's quiet.

Hub was starting to get fidgety when Elise put the book down. She yawned, then slowly unbuttoned her sweater. Action at last. But not the kind Hub wanted to see. Spying didn't excite him, nor did invading a woman's privacy while she undressed, even if she happened to be attractive. Hub felt uncomfortable. He wasn't getting a professional payoff here. The stakeout made him little more than a Peeping Tom.

Elise's skirt dropped to the floor. Her attitude unself-conscious, almost languid, she strolled to the window and looked out into the night.

Directly into Hub's binoculars.

For a moment he was sure she'd spotted him. Somehow, she'd zeroed right in.

But that was impossible. Deep shadows concealed him; his coat had to be blending in. Furthermore, the binoculars' lenses were laminated to prevent reflections; no way could she have the slightest clue he stood there watching. Hub didn't believe in psychic abilities. Nonetheless, he felt a weird stab of unease. Did Elise have X-ray eyes?

Her gaze strayed, surveying other elements of the nightscape. Windows, roofs, fire escapes, places, Hub realized, from which someone could view her apartment. Which was to say, places like the spot in which he stood. Hub realized something else. Of course Elise couldn't see him.

But she knew that he, or someone in his employ, was out there somewhere. And she wasn't at all shy about advertising that fact.

The next morning Hub entered the Federal Building, took the elevator up, and headed for his office. As he approached, his secretary, Janeen, tossed her chin within. Someone was waiting there.

Hub recognized the visitor. Clad in a well-tailored suit, fit, and effortlessly charismatic, he was General William Devereaux.

"Hi," said the general. "I understand they call you Hub."

"I know who you are," Hub replied, masking his surprise.

Devereaux extended his hand. "Bill Devereaux," he said affably, establishing an informal tone.

Hub shook the man's hand, and said, "I served in the . . ."

Devereaux interrupted. "In the 82nd Airborne, I know. Same time I was running the 173rd."

Both men took seats. "Put me through school," Hub remarked.

Devereaux's eyes twinkled, with something more than good humor. As if addressing an assemblage, not an FBI ASAC, he declaimed, *"God. Duty. Honor. Country.* Where on Capitol Hill, Wall Street, or Hollywood would you find one man who's even paused over one of those words in the last ten years?"

Hub had paused over the words in question quite a lot over the last ten years, and knew more than a few others who had as well. He didn't point that out. General Devereaux wasn't putting on this command performance to elicit debate. "What, uh, brings you here, General?" Hub inquired. "Can I get you some coffee?"

"You want me to get to the point," Devereaux observed. "The president's concerned. He's worried that . . . have you met him by any chance?"

Hub suppressed a smile. Of course he hadn't met the president. Even if he had, the occasion wouldn't have shed any more light on the president's concerns than what Hub saw on the news. "I know," Hub said, groping for a reply, "reading the papers, that terrorism's a real concern for him. And your job is to—"

Again Devereaux interrupted. "With all the affection for the man," he said brusquely, "I can tell you he doesn't know fuck-all about terrorism, or the Mideast, that I don't put on his cue cards. What he's expert in is his own survival. You get my meaning?"

No, Hub thought. He had begun to wonder if the general could be softening him up for some news about a change in jurisdiction over the #87 bus. He said carefully, "I didn't guess you came all this way for a cup of coffee."

"Agent *Hubbard,*" Devereaux cried, the twinkles now blazing from his eyes, "you look like you think I'm here to take your baby away!"

Hub held his ground. "With all respect for your expertise, sir. I think we're on track here. I want to complete my mission."

"Which is what I said to the president," Devereaux said smoothly. "The army is not some big green police department. Stick with the man on the ground."

Hub said, "I appreciate your support."

Devereaux cocked his head thoughtfully. "You're sure you're not chasing your own tail, though?"

Uh-oh, Hub thought. He considered the question for a moment, then asked, "What do you know about Sheik Ahmed bin Talal?"

"Old news," Devereaux said dismissively.

"Maybe not," Hub replied. "We've received two communications—we believe from the bombers—'Release him.'"

"We can't release him," Devereaux said.

Hub misunderstood the general's drift. He said, "I know our stated policy is not to negotiate with terrorists, but . . ."

"Hub," Devereaux cut in, "we can't release him because we don't have him. We never had him. And besides that, he's dead."

Hub frowned. "The CIA says . . ."

"The CIA?" Devereaux interrupted; a frequent habit, Hub noted. "The CIA couldn't predict the fall of the Berlin Wall until bricks were hitting them in the head."

True, Hub thought.

"The Libyans snatched the sheik," Devereaux continued. "Some sectarian Muslim thing—I'll explain it the next time you have a free week. They killed him. Qaddafi put out disinformation that it was us." Hard eyes scanned Hub's face. "Who was your source on this?"

"Elise Kraft," Hub replied.

Devereaux shook his head. "A woman will never know the Middle East," he declared. "You're talking about a culture that keeps its women slipcovered. Elise Kraft can't tell a sheik from the prophylactic of the same name."

Hub murmured, "I appreciate the heads-up." The general's certitude didn't convince him, however. First, it seemed a little too practiced, as if Devereaux had anticipated Hub's question about bin Talal. Second, why hadn't Devereaux expressed even the slightest interest in the "Release him" demand? Could the demand really be that insignificant? Or did it mean something that Devereaux wanted to keep quiet?

Devereaux rose, offering his hand. As they shook, a head peered into the office; no knock gave notice. Hub turned and saw Elise.

She said, "Hub, we've got Judge Frankel in . . ." General Devereaux also turned to face her. "Oh," Elise said expressionlessly. "Hello, General."

Devereaux waved a hand, urging Elise to carry on with her business. "Please, don't let me . . ."

"Sorry," she said to Hub. "That tip on the landlord looks solid. The judge will see us right away."

"Sounds like I should get out of your way," Devereaux remarked. He moved to the door. "Your father well, Elise?" he inquired politely.

"As can be expected," Elise replied. "How's Maggie?"

"Top of her game," Devereaux said with a breezy smile. "Well, go get 'em," he added as he swept through the door.

Elise said to Hub, "Making new friends?"

Hub, ignoring the question, looked at Elise's mouth. "What happened to your lip?" he asked.

He already knew, of course. The bruise had come courtesy of Samir. Elise, quick on the uptake, saw that he knew this. They eyed each other, without words acknowledging the surveillance that Elise so obviously had suspected while looking out her window the night before.

"So," she said, brazening it out. "You like to watch?"

"No," Hub said with a poker face. "Just learning about commitment."

"It's a full-contact sport," Elise said.

She's a tough one, Hub thought. *Doesn't give an inch.*

13

Judge Abraham Frankel received Hub and Elise in his chambers at the Federal Courthouse in downtown Brooklyn. Age sixty, he'd devoted his adult life to serving the law in one capacity or another, and thus had heard just about every story under the jurisprudential sun. Including Hub's.

The judge set down his midmorning sandwich and wiped his hands. "You're telling me," he said skeptically, "that just because some Brooklyn landlord tips you off that he's been paid in cash, you have the right to call in the cavalry? Hub, as far as I know, paying *cash* is not yet a crime in this country."

"You're not hearing me," Hub replied. "This Khalil was carrying cash for—"

"You've observed him giving cash?" Frankel demanded. "To whom?"

"No," Hub conceded. "But . . ."

"But you have hard evidence," Frankel suggested, not believing a word of it. "Linking this apartment to the people that blew up Bus 87?"

Elise sat quietly next to Hub, aware that contributions from her wouldn't improve Frankel's view of their request. For one thing the judge could ask about her bureaucratic provenance, and if informed of its exact nature, might well decide that Hub stood on even shakier legal ground. Although the Cooperation Agreement spelled out in Special Order 12333 did permit the CIA to participate in domestic cases involving foreign terrorists, the Agreement's fine points remained controversial. Few people wanted to give the CIA the latitude it enjoyed overseas. Jurists of Frankel's generation tended to remember, not fondly, the domestic counterintelligence scandals of the seventies—episodes in which the Agency had played a number of roles.

Hub said, "I know we'll turn up trace elements of Semtex, chemicals . . ." His voice trailed off. "Something," he added. His left ear was bothering him. Most of the time he could ignore the tinnitus, but at the moment his hearing was off-kilter. The words he'd just spoken sounded far away, and lame.

"And when you do, you'll get your warrant," the judge said firmly.

"What about a feasibility study?" Hub asked. A shot in the dark. He doubted it would work.

"Meaning?" the judge inquired, his lined face leery.

"We enter first, take a look, then fill out a warrant," Hub replied. He put on his most wholesome Boy Scout demeanor, which didn't require a lot of effort. Actually, Hub had to work fairly hard not to look the very picture of innocence.

Frankel didn't buy it. He said, "Tell me the difference between that and breaking and entering?"

"We're the good guys," Hub said evenly.

"Not good enough," Frankel declared.

"What *is* good enough?" Hub demanded. "Another bus? A school, maybe?" The judge frowned at him. "These things come in waves," Hub warned.

"Waves mean nothing to me," Frankel said decisively. "There's been a continuous wave of muggings in this city for the last forty years, but if you came to me with a plan to put all muggers behind bars as a preventative measure, I'd send you packing." Hub knew what was coming next; it always came next. "There's a price to be paid," Frankel admonished, confirming Hub's expectation down to the last syllable, "for living in a free society."

Hub replied, "And not in cash, I guarantee it."

He caught Elise's eye. They were going nowhere. Time to get the hell out.

*   *   *

Fifteen minutes later Hub and Elise climbed the stairwell of a squalid Brooklyn tenement. They hadn't said much to each other during the drive over; Frankel's hard line had dampened their moods. But the stairwell was enlivening Elise. It seemed endless. Much like their quest to find the bombers. "Not two judges from now," she was saying with unusual vehemence. "Not two *hours* from now, not two *minutes* from now, these guys could split any *second* and you've lost your best shot at . . ."

"Frank's working on another warrant," Hub reminded her.

Elise exclaimed, "You don't understand, they're pros! From the age of twelve they've been dodging people like you, people *better* than you!"

"You mean people like you?" Hub asked acidly.

Their feet tramped up the concrete steps, generating raspy echoes. Elise hadn't yet come to terms with Frankel's decision. She wanted to believe that they could somehow circumvent it and was doing her best to get Hub on board. "No matter how sparkling your record is," she told him. "No matter how terrified you are to fail . . ."

Now she was starting to draw blood. Hub halted abruptly and turned. Measuring out his words, putting intervals between them to telegraph their import, he said, "It's—against—the—*law*."

Elise glared at him, her temper closer to the surface than Hub heretofore had seen. A fiery red-head, showing claws, she said caustically, "Just because you went to night school, or filled out the back of a matchbook or whatever you did to get a law degree, doesn't make you Sir Thomas More."

Hub's own temper flared. "Just because *you* talk the talk doesn't make you an expert. And just because you read my file doesn't make you an expert on *me*."

He resumed climbing the stairs. Elise followed. She told his backside, "You're gonna lose them, and they're gonna do another horrible . . ."

Hub snapped, "You think I *want* to lose them? Where do you get off talking that shit?" For a moment it was touch-and-go; Elise had gotten under his skin. Hub steadied himself by focusing on the endless steps. He said, "If I don't take 'em down properly, they'll be on the street two hours from now. I could find dynamite, Semtex, pluto-nium, and a book of matches in there, and unless I've got the right warrant, it's *all inadmissible*."

"They've also got a *warrant*," Elise replied. "A warrant from God. They're ready to *die*!" She panted as they rounded another landing, a bit out of breath. "And your quaint laws don't mean shit to these people."

"*My* quaint laws?" Hub expostulated. "Last I checked you were an American citizen. And these happen to be the only laws we got." Again he stopped and whirled. "Look," he said intently, "I'm real sorry the cold war's over, and you Masters of the Universe got nothing going on over there in Afghanistan or Iraq or wherever—but you're just not in the Middle East anymore."

"Oh, really?" Elise said, the sarcasm in her voice challenging Hub's last statement. She'd been trying to get it through his skull that they truly were in alien territory here. Even if the map did say it was Brooklyn.

Hub trudged to stairwell's top. A surprise stood around the corner. Frank Haddad, a document dangling from his hand. Hub drank it in. *Damn,* he thought. *The warrant.*

Frank had listened to the argument echoing up the stairwell. He expected double takes from his partners when they saw what he held; their reactions didn't disappoint him. Frank grinned at the staring faces.

Within half an hour they'd set up surveillance equipment in a room that looked out on another apartment building, equally squalid, across the street. That building held their target: an apartment the windows of which were screened by paper shades. Elise, wearing headphones, used an audio probe to catch voices beyond the shades. Frank operated an infrared device that detected heat emanating from human bodies.

Hub, meanwhile, conferred with the target building's landlord. Syrian by background, his cooperation hadn't been a foregone conclusion. Once apprised of the reason for the investigation, however, he'd proved more than eager to help. Like the *mullah* who had spoken at the mosque the evening before, he saw no justification in the Koran for blowing bus passengers to bits. Quite the contrary. Not only did the bombing violate his moral sensibilities. It jeopardized the good standing of Muslims all across America.

Elise removed her headset. "They're discussing how hard it is to find a decent cup of coffee," she told Frank. She passed the headset to him. "I make out three voices. What do you have on the infrared?"

"Three sounds right," Frank replied. "If we had microwave, we'd know for sure." He looked at her reproachfully. "The CIA's got microwave; how come we don't have microwave?"

Elise shrugged. Frank had a point; without going to much trouble she could have rustled up some of the revolutionary new microwave eavesdropping technology. But fancy toys didn't strike her as the key to cracking this case. Human assets were her forte; and anyway, the old equipment worked fine as far as she was concerned. It was getting results right there.

"Three of them," the landlord was telling Hub.

"All day long they watch TV. And eat pizza. Nothing but pizza, pizza, pizza."

Hub and Frank exchanged glances. The suspects' dietary taste provided a way in.

Mike Johannson, wearing delivery garb and carrying two boxed pizzas, climbed the never-ending stairs of the tenement building. He reached a dark hallway, walked down it, and knocked on a door.

In the shadows of the landing below him a small army of FBI agents readied their weapons.

The door opened three inches, pulling taut a security chain on the other side. A young Arab, barely out of his teens, pushed a twenty-dollar bill through the crack.

Mike said, "You want change, right?"

"No," the youth said, his voice heavily accented.

"You gonna open the door or what?" Mike demanded, doing a fair imitation of an offended pizza guy.

The Arab gestured at the floor. As far as he was concerned, the delivery stopped there.

"Jesus," Mike said. "Didn't ya hear crime's down seven percent?" Muttering to himself, he set the boxes on the floor and headed back downstairs.

After his footfalls had faded, the security chain rattled. The FBI team listened to the door creak open, then creak shut. Its locks turned.

The apartment was sparsely furnished. The

Arab placed the pizza boxes on an orange crate that served as a table. In the next room two other young Arabs were glued to a TV set playing a rerun of *Hunter*. Though hungry enough, they weren't going to divide their attention until the episode climaxed.

The young man who'd paid for the pizza liked to eat it hot. He got more than he'd bargained for. When he opened the top box he triggered the stun grenade hidden within. A blinding flash erupted, flinging him to the floor.

An instant later the apartment's front door also erupted. Agents stormed in through billowing smoke, guns pointed, Hub leading the way. Voices shouted in both English and Arabic: *"FBI! Lie down on the floor with your hands behind your backs!"*

The *Hunter* rerun minimized the stun grenade's effects on the other young men. A doorway separated them from the blast; furthermore, they hadn't been looking in its direction. Their vision intact, their reflexes quick, they responded to the invasion with a blaze of gunfire.

Not quickly enough. Each got off less than half a clip before an FBI fusillade cut them down.

The stunned Arab rose shakily to his feet, blinking, shaking his head. He gaped at the business ends of six guns pointed at his chest.

Frank yelled, "Drop your weapon!"

The youth stared with empty eyes. His right

hand clutched a pistol; in his dazed state he couldn't use it against the agents faster than they could fill him with lead. Given the covenants that governed his mission, he had only one option. He stuck the gun in his mouth and pulled the trigger.

His head jerked backward, spewing bone and brains. Cordite eddied lazily to the ceiling; the boy thumped onto the floor.

Hub called from his position beyond a table, "What about the others? See if we can get a pulse!"

Agents rushed to the still bodies. "Terminal," Fred Darius reported, his fingers finding nothing in a limp wrist.

"Same here," Mike Johannson said from the other corpse.

"Gone," Elise said quietly. Hub glimpsed her kneeling beside the kid who'd just blown his head apart. She had placed her hand on his boyish chest. A kind of tenderness motivated the gesture, Hub realized. Tenderness mingled with profound regret.

Mike Johannson conducted a quick survey of the apartment. "We got Semtex," he announced, "we got detcord, same stuff as the bus, the whole enchilada."

Whoops and high fives greeted the news. None of the agents enjoyed causing death, far from it. At the same time, firefights always produced an adrenaline rush that required release.

Pent-up tension abated. Frank opened the second pizza box. "Anybody like anchovies?" he asked the room with genial good humor.

Hub did. But he'd just noticed something that took his breath away. An object rested on the floor near the blown-out front door. Hub knelt beside it. The squat shape and gunmetal color identified it as a device capable of destroying the entire apartment and considerable regions beyond: a claymore mine.

"Goddamn," Hub said softly as he checked the mine's wiring, where the wiring went. "*Goddamn it!*" he bellowed.

"What?" Frank blurted, geniality draining from his face.

Hub gestured at the claymore. "It didn't fire," he said with utter incredulity. "They had it rigged to the door, and it didn't fire."

The lethal booby trap riveted Frank and the other agents. Hub shook his head. "We're too old to be lucky, Frank," he muttered.

Elise stared at the mine. For once, she and Hub agreed.

14

That night the FBI takedown team gathered at a SoHo bar. Loud music and residual nerves inspired Mike Johannson and Tina Osu to cut loose on the small dance floor. Other agents surrounded them, drinking, laughing, blowing off steam. Fred Darius and Danny Sussman eyed the dancing couple appreciatively, and not without envy. What had Mike done to deserve raising such hell with Tina?

Hub and Elise sat at a nearby table watching the revelry. Elise sipped her drink. "My first boyfriend was Palestinian," she remarked. "My father liked to say, they seduce you with their suffering."

Hub remembered the tenderness with which Elise had touched the Arab boy who'd opened his last box of pizza. She seemed to have considerable empathy for the downtrodden of that part of the world. Hub wondered if it sometimes got in her way. Possibly, he decided. Maybe even likely.

"You ever been over there?" Elise asked.

Hub shook his head. Part of him doubted he ever would get over there. FBI business might make it happen someday. Other than that, he couldn't think of a reason.

"The courtesy with which they welcome you into their homes," Elise said, fondly reminiscent. "And the people, these incredibly *warm* people in this . . ." Her eyes clouded. "Austere land."

"But you work against them," Hub commented. An image flashed through his mind: Khalil, his face empurpled with bruises, sitting in the basement den of the otherwise empty Brooklyn house. Elise, hard as nails, facing him from the BarcaLounger.

"Only the crazies," Elise replied. "I tend to be suspicious of all true believers." She cocked her head at Hub, a touch tipsily. "Present company included," she added.

Hub's mouth curled with the beginnings of a smile. "So I'm a fanatic?" he inquired. For some reason the idea amused him. He didn't feel like a fanatic.

"Let's just say you don't seem the ambivalent type," Elise said.

"Is that right?" Hub said, intrigued now. What was Elise getting at here?

As if proving her case, she answered with a question. "So why are you a Fed?"

"That's what my nephew keeps asking me," Hub confessed. "'Why you with The Man, Unc?'" he quoted, homeboy-style.

"Well . . . ?" Elise prodded, her face less severe than usual. Openly curious, too. She really wants to know, Hub realized with surprise. "What'd you tell him?" she asked.

Hub reviewed the various ways he'd tried to explain the FBI to his nephew. None of Elise's business, he decided; something inside him clicked shut. "You read my file," he said, curious about what Elise had seen. "You tell me." He gave her a quizzical stare. Maybe she would tell him something he didn't know about his decision to pursue a career with the FBI.

"Let's see," Elise said reflectively, accessing a mental database. "Catholic school. Captain of this, president of that. Hard work, fair play, make a difference, change the system from within." She smiled with a trace of derision. "Rah, rah, rah."

"That was in my file?" Hub asked, a bit ruffled.

"'Tell me I'm wrong," Elise rejoined.

It seemed like a dare. One that Hub wasn't sure he wanted to take. While Elise's thumbnail sketch sounded fair enough as far as it went, pointing out its limitations would require delving into areas he didn't much want to share. How well did he know this woman? He studied her, understanding for the first time, a little uneasily, that his curiosity about

Elise wasn't confined to the impact she'd been making on his professional life. She interested him on a deeper level: He wanted to know what made her tick. Again he recalled Khalil's bruised face. Whatever it was that made Elise Kraft tick had some serious dimensions. Who, really, was Elise Kraft?

"What?" she demanded as Hub's stare lengthened.

"You believe in anything, Elise?" he asked.

"Like what, for instance?" she replied tartly.

"How about right and wrong?" Hub suggested.

Elise waved a hand, and declared, "It's easy to choose between right and wrong. What's hard is choosing the wrong that's more right." She sighed. "I just want to make it all . . . a little . . . better." She drained her drink. "Ignore me," she said with self-deprecating joviality. "I'm shit-faced."

Frank leaned over their table. "So am I!" he brayed, always the party clown. "Hey, Elise," he added teasingly, "tell us about being a spook? Ever meet Aldrich Ames?" Elise smiled; she happened to have a few stories to tell about the self-obsessed dipso, but not here. "Weren't you at the Bay of Pigs?" Frank persisted, grinning, his tone more impish than mocking.

"You were in charge of Waco, right?" Elise countered. "Or was that Ruby Ridge?"

"The Shah of Iran, Noriega, I love the way you guys predicted the collapse of the Soviet Union,"

Frank went on, counting down the pratfalls. His litany delighted him.

"Yeah, yeah, yeah," Elise said, dryly dismissive. "And J. Edgar Hoover wore a dress." She laughed and got to her feet, with a sweep of her hand inviting Hub to dance. "What do you say, Hub?" she said. "Peace?"

Grudgingly, Hub stood. As former captain of this and former president of that, he couldn't very well refuse a lady's invitation to dance, could he? No, that would be callow. Not at all *rah rah rah*.

But right then the music changed. A slow ballad came on. *Shit*, thought Hub, unprepared for physical contact with Elise. Dancing at a distance was one thing; up-close-and-personal was another. They stood there awkwardly for a moment, each aware of the situation's comic dimension.

Frank beamed at them, hugely amused.

Finally, Hub took Elise in his arms. As they moved onto the dance floor, eliciting the inevitable bright-eyed stares and muted snickers, Elise remarked, "This feels like high school."

"Only my prom date wasn't packing a gun," Hub recalled.

"Mine's a nine millimeter," Elise volunteered. "How big is yours?"

"Two inches," Hub growled. "From the ground." They both laughed. The ice broke; they found themselves dancing closer, with more ease.

"So what's the latest from Samir?" Hub asked, seeing no reason not to mix business with frivolity. "I want a list of every visa he sponsored."

"Not sure he'll do it," Elise murmured.

And why is that? Hub asked himself. *Because Elise's empathy for Samir was getting in her way?* He remarked, "I once knew this undercover guy, started to care so much about his source . . ."

"Samir's a source," Elise said flatly. "Period."

"Have you considered that he might also be in bed with the other side?" Hub asked.

"Samir in bed with them?" Elise said, disbelief flashing from her eyes. "That would be too much to ask for."

"You're so confident," Hub observed.

"Only in bed," Elise quipped.

Tina drank in the sight of the ASAC dancing with the redheaded spook. Drolly, she rolled her eyes at Frank. Tina knew better than anyone that Hub was overdue for some girl action. But with Elise?

Frank was about to offer his take on the issue when the floor moved. It actually shook; a low rumble throbbed through. Lights flickered as chandeliers swayed. The ballad missed a couple of beats; in highball glasses that hands weren't touching, ice clinked.

"*Whoa,*" Frank exclaimed. "What *do* they put in these drinks?"

Tina said with disbelief, "They got earthquakes in Manhattan?

Elise disengaged herself from Hub and swiftly made her way to the door. *She isn't all that shitfaced,* Hub noted as he joined her. The nighttime street scene looked okay apart from the not-so-insignificant fact that everyone in sight had frozen. The apparent seismic event hadn't been confined to the bar. Up and down the block, nonplussed pedestrians were trying to figure it out.

From a distance, well uptown, Hub and Elise heard sirens wailing. They stared at each other, sharing an instantaneous realization: Those sirens would only multiply, only get louder. Something enormous had just happened.

Frank joined them on the sidewalk. "Let's go," Hub barked, heading for his car.

They sped up Madison Avenue, grimly keeping their thoughts to themselves, the car's blue light flashing. At Thirty-seventh Street the traffic thickened and slowed; by Fortieth it had congealed into gridlock. The sirens were indeed multiplying, but their wails now competed with another loud noise: hundreds of honking horns.

The gridlock wouldn't go away anytime soon, Hub could see at a glance. He opened his door and set out on foot through a honking sea of immobilized cars. The anger of the people in them fueled his sense of urgency; this situation would deteriorate if it posed an ongoing threat to civilians and required an evacuation. *God, not that,* Hub thought feverishly. He had participated in contingency planning for responses to bioweapon attacks, and knew the city's chief weak point: simply getting people away. Hub broke into a run. Elise and Frank followed, weaving between stalled trucks, buses, and cars.

Hub headed west to Broadway and turned north on it, using various sounds and gut instinct to home in on whatever had happened. The sounds weren't pretty; shouts and screams had begun to filter through the sirens, the horns. As he neared Forty-second Street he knew he was getting close. Then he turned the corner. And saw it.

Smoke poured into the night from the New Victory Theater, the venerable showcase that had pioneered the revitalization of city's entertainment district. Even Hub's practiced eye couldn't get an immediate grip on what was going on. He saw limousines at odd angles to the sidewalk, as if they'd been shoved aside. He saw flashing lights, chaos, dazed people in expensive evening clothes. And then he saw the girl walking toward him.

She wore a gorgeous couture gown. She held a jeweled clutch bag, the kind society women take to the opera; a tasteful necklace adorned her neck. A stunning girl, perfect in every way, except for the horror radiating from her eyes—and the fact that *her right arm was missing*.

It had to have been severed just minutes before. Only shock kept her on her feet. Any moment, the girl would collapse.

Hub blinked at her, nausea spiraling up from his stomach, through his torso. The law-enforcement sector of his mind took over; it gave him detachment, an ability to catalog the realities before him. Cop cars were parking haphazardly on the theater's steps. Firemen unspooled hoses from blinking trucks. Bystanders stood still, unable to respond to the mayhem. Victims milled about screaming their heads off, waving shattered limbs, tearing at bloodied clothes. A woman's gown had incinerated into her skin; she appeared unaware of that fact. As Hub watched, she collapsed into a lifeless heap. Cops, firefighters, and emergency medical technicians ran around every which way, seemingly at random, but Hub could see that under the circumstances they were functioning with discipline. Though as horrified as anyone else, they'd been trained to deal with sudden catastrophe. The training showed.

Hub raced forward, Elise keeping pace beside him. They passed a man in formal black-tie attire; he quietly wept below one of the formidable stone lions that abutted the theater's front staircase. Less lucky survivors stumbled on the steps, their faces chopped up and bleeding, their elegant clothing in shreds. A high-end gala must have been under way in the theater, Hub concluded. Probably a benefit for some worthy cause, no doubt celebrity-studded. He caught himself thinking: *They'll be printing the obituaries for weeks.*

A shrill sound filled the air, one Hub didn't recognize at first as human in origin. A kind of keening.

Elise had heard the sound before. But only in places such as Jerusalem and Beirut—never in the United States. People keened like this when grief and rage merged. The grief derived from their lives' having been ripped apart. The rage derived from lives having been ripped apart recently before, in this case on a bus, establishing a pattern, and derived also from an appalling fear that it would happen again, and again, with nothing in sight to stop it.

Hub approached an NYPD sergeant, the senior officer on the scene. A bit shell-shocked, the man nodded blankly as Hub showed his shield. He muttered, "Fucking bastards waited 'til intermission. Everybody standing around." His lips trembled. "Oh, Jesus," he moaned, at a loss for words.

Glass crunched underfoot as emergency personnel hurried up and down the steps. Hub felt helpless as EMTs brought out stretchers holding horribly disfigured victims. Glaring lights approached, the vanguard of a rapid-response TV news team. *Great*, thought Hub. A reporter stuck a microphone in his face, and asked, "Is it true the governor was attending tonight's benefit?"

"I don't know," Hub replied. An insight was dawning on him. If this were the work of the same terrorist organization that had hit the #87 bus— and Hub had little doubt that it was—the conflict would continue to escalate in hideous ways. No one pulled off a hit like this unless prepared to take it even further. What would come next? City Hall? An ocean liner? A skyscraper?

"Who is it I'm speaking to?" the reporter demanded.

Hub ignored him. He noticed that Elise had knelt and was ripping up part of her skirt, improvising bandages to dress the wounds of a society matron who lay twitching beside her. The lady needed the attention. She was bleeding badly.

Only one thing to do. Hub took off his coat, joined Elise, and went to work.

15

Hub stretched his limbs in the darkened airplane cabin, grateful that no one else shared his row. He was contending with overload; the atrocities he'd seen, heard, and smelled at the New Victory Theater left an ineradicable burn in his mind, his heart. Along with Elise and Frank and dozens of other FBI personnel who had expected to enjoy a night off following the terrorist takedown, he'd stayed on-site for hours, first helping to stabilize the survivors, then establishing a framework for the forensics investigation that lay ahead. Detcord, Semtex, the telltale benzene spike—those items and more had to be found, confirmed, cross-checked in the mainframe, then confirmed again.

All of which added up to no sleep. Only Hub's solid constitution was keeping him going. He couldn't have slept in any case, not even aboard the plane. On top of his accelerated mental state, churning with memories of slaughter, the departure from La Guardia had triggered terrible pain in his ears; air pressure variations exacerbated the damage from Bus 87's sonic blast. Hub's head was still throbbing more than forty minutes after take-off. For the time being, at any rate, sleep was out of the question.

He wasn't going to worry about it. More important problems confronted him. The closest at hand concerned the meeting to which a phone call had summoned him. Hub had no idea what would be decided at the meeting. Worse, he suspected nobody else knew, either.

The pilot's voice came over the intercom: "Folks, as you can probably tell, we have begun our descent into Reagan National Airport."

Uh-oh, thought Hub, feeling pressure build in his ears as the plane banked lower. He knew right away that this time the pain would hit harder. A high-pitched whistling sound coursed from his eardrums through his sinuses. It reminded him of the sound that had whited out his hearing when the bus exploded. He then realized that it was the *same* sound—for some reason coming back.

It got louder, then louder still. Grimacing, Hub reached for his ears. He couldn't take this; perspiration trickled down his ribs. As had happened following the explosion, the sound reached a limit beyond which he was sure it couldn't possibly rise, only to amplify yet more, as if in geometric progression. It punched through into a new acoustical realm—unbearably more pure, unbearably more loud—a harmonic fusion that seemed to white out the plane, the seat, even the stewardess . . .

The stewardess loomed over him, her face taut with concern. Hub watched her lips move. But he couldn't hear the words issuing from them. He concentrated, trying to lip-read. "You all right?" she was mouthing.

Hub didn't know how to reply. He couldn't reply; awash with sweat, he gripped his armrests, praying the pressure would subside.

And then, against the excruciating field of noise, somehow bleeding through it, Hub heard the words of the army general whose phone call had put him on this plane. *"Either we solve this threat quickly and convincingly,"* the general had told him, his voice strained, *"or next week there'll be a hundred more all over the world."*

The Capitol's dome gleamed under early-morning sun. Hub walked up the enormous staircase in a fresh suit. He'd napped fitfully for a couple of hours at a hotel and taken a long shower. Apart from residue buzz in his ears, more an irritant now than real pain, he almost felt whole again.

The security people at the rotunda entrance were expecting him. Somewhat to his surprise, they wanted to see his shield, Bureau classification clearance, and driver's license—measures they weren't requiring of the tourists passing through the checkpoint's metal detectors. Hub noted the extra personnel posted at the door and along the lobby. This happened to be the first time he'd visited the Capitol since a paranoid schizophrenic had gunned down two guards, the only such fatalities in the history of the great building. As with so many other incidents of recent years, the tragedy had left its mark. No one's benign intentions could be taken for granted.

He followed two guards across the rotunda, then through a restricted area, and finally to a tall wooden door. When it opened, revealing the officials who sat around a gleaming table in an astonishingly ornate library—carved woodwork, marble busts on pedestals, heavily framed oil paintings by American masters, gold leaf everywhere—Hub understood why the guards out front had needed to see three pieces of ID. He'd just been admitted to the highest echelons of American governmental power.

General Devereaux chaired the meeting. In terms of protocol, however, he ranked as the most junior figure at the table. *Except for me,* Hub hastily corrected himself. Then he realized that he wouldn't be sitting at the table, and could understand why: He'd never before seen in person such a concentration of heavyweights. The directors of the FBI and the CIA. The attorney general. The Speaker of the House. Todd Franklin, the White House chief of staff. Senator Clarence Wright, chairman of the Foreign Relations Committee. Congressman Fred Marshall, the majority whip. And, finally, a four-star army general whom Hub didn't recognize but who probably wielded clout beyond his stars. Hub had heard stories about senior military people who deliberately kept a low public profile. They were the ones you watched out for; relative anonymity gave them latitude for dirty work, work that could sometimes be exceedingly dirty indeed.

The general was saying, "Or soon there'll be hundreds more like it everywhere in sight."

Hub recognized the voice. He'd heard it over the phone at 3:00 A.M. that day, instructing him to get on a plane. The door closed silently behind him; other elements in the room caught his attention. A plethora of staff people either stood along walls or were seated in chairs at a respectful remove from the table, holding clipboards, briefcases, valises stuffed with documents. Telephones that looked as if they'd just been installed sat on a wheeled cart. A couple of computer workstations discreetly hummed. The sterling silver coffee-service array, attended by a uniformed steward, could have been an exhibit in a museum.

Denzel Washington stars as FBI Special Agent Anthony "Hub" Hubbard.

Hub tries to negotiate with the terrorists holding the city bus: ". . . let the rest of the passengers go, and I'll take their place . . ."

Without warning the bus explodes, killing everyone on board. It is only the beginning of "the siege."

Hub, deafened by the bomb blast, tries to tell his friend, FBI Agent Frank Haddad (played by Tony Shalhoub), that he isn't hurt.

Annette Bening plays Sharon Bridger, a beautiful CIA operative with mysterious connections to Islamic revolutionaries. Her contacts may be the key to stopping the terror.

As the terrorist attacks escalate, Hub is called to a high-powered, emergency summit in Washington, D.C.

Hub argues passionately against calling in the army to establish a state of martial law.

Hub and Haddad track Sharon's movements as she surreptitiously visits a Brooklyn mosque.

The terror and bloodshed continue as the terrorists bomb the Federal Building in New York, home of the FBI offices.

Hub and Sharon together persuade her contact, Samir, to give them the crucial name that will lead the FBI to the next terrorist cell.

Hub works late into the night on the case. If he doesn't find an answer soon, it will be too late—for everyone.

Almost against their will, Hub and Sharon draw closer together as they work night and day to find the terrorists.

Hub confronts Devereaux. Under the new martial law, Frank Haddad's thirteen-year-old son has been taken in for questioning.

Hub to Devereaux:
"... What if they
don't want their leader back at all. ... Maybe what they
really want is that we herd our children into stadiums.
Put soldiers on our streets. Bend the law, shred the
constitution. Then the country men like us have sworn
to defend, and bled to defend, and died to defend ... is
gone. And they've won."

New York City is under full-scale martial law. All constitutional rights have been revoked by order of the President.

The final terrorist holds Sharon at gunpoint. Hub confronts him: "Let her go and you'll live."

Congressman Marshall cleared his throat. He said, replying to the four-star, "Sounds great, General. Except why can't we find out who's behind it?"

The FBI director leaned forward, acknowledging that the congressman's question was directed in part at him. "These sects are organized so you need a kill to your credit to get inside," he explained. "It makes undercover operations impossible. What that leaves us with . . ." He shook his head, frustration etched on his face. "We're working on it."

Senator Wright demanded, "How about who's behind whoever is behind this?"

"Libya," the CIA director said speculatively, without conviction. "Iraq. Iran. Possibly Syria."

"Ask a question," observed Todd Franklin, the White House chief of staff, "get an atlas." His tone made clear his lack of confidence in the proceedings.

Senator Wright snapped, "All I know is that we *must* respond."

"Respond, sure," Todd Franklin shot back. "But how?"

Senator Wright said impatiently, "Find out who it is and bomb the shit out of them."

"And if we can't find out?" Franklin asked. His raised eyebrows lent force to the question. It hung disagreeably in the air.

Congressman Marshall broke the silence.

"Look, it keeps escalating," he complained. "First a bus, then the theater. What's next?"

"Anything but leadership," Senator Wright said darkly.

"With all due respect, Senator," General Devereaux interjected, his chiseled face serious but radiating charm. "Why don't we just stipulate that the president is a dumb son of a bitch so we can all get down to business?"

Devereaux's comment broke the ice; chuckles washed through the room. Even Todd Franklin, of those present the closest to the president, permitted himself a smile.

"What about sending in the Guard?" Congressman Marshall suggested.

The attorney general said firmly, her schoolmarmish face brooking no nonsense, "The National Guard are trained for riot control. Not counterterrorism."

"The army then," Senator Wright said. "I've seen the contingency plans."

"It's settled legal doctrine," the attorney general replied. "*Posse comitatus.* The army must not be turned against our own people."

Senator Wright regarded the attorney general through heavy-lidded eyes. "Even if that's what our own people are asking for, three-to-one?"

The Speaker of the House spoke up. "If the president," he conjectured, his face animating as he considered the possibility, "is willing to declare a state of emergency . . . ?"

Senator Wright snorted. "President *Lincoln* declared martial law in 1862," he said. "He suspended . . ."

"Which the Supreme Court later found unconstitutional," the attorney general interrupted. "*Ex parte Milligan*."

"And I've got an election in November," Congressman Marshall replied. "*Ex*–United States congressman."

"Guys, guys," Todd Franklin intervened. "The president lost a lot of friends last night."

"Not to mention three points in the polls," Congressman Marshall noted.

Franklin ignored Marshall's disrespect. "And his plane lands in two hours," the chief of staff went on. "We owe it to him to have a consensus."

The Speaker of the House remarked, his jowls aquiver, "You don't fight a junkyard dog with ASPCA rules. What you do is take the leash off your own bigger, meaner dog."

Heads nodded around the table. The Speaker had given voice to a sentiment they all shared to one degree or another. Todd Franklin gazed at General Devereaux. Who just might be the biggest, meanest dog available, Hub reflected. The general had served for some time as the president's point man on terrorism. Not only had he studied the problem from historical and academic points of view. He'd also mounted a number of successful clandestine operations—some of which, rumor had it, have never been disclosed, not even to senior Administration figures. "General?" Franklin said to Devereaux, inviting comment.

"The army is a broadsword, not a scalpel," Devereaux said succinctly. "You do *not* want us in an American city."

"But hypothetically," Franklin said, his intelligent face composed, urging Devereaux to reconsider. "How long would it take you to—"

"We only go in if the president invokes the War Powers Act," Devereaux declared.

"I understand that, General," Franklin replied. "Let us imagine, though, for a moment, that the order has been given."

A stir circled the table as the participants thought it over. One by one, they looked expectantly at Devereaux. If anyone could spell out the consequences of such a scenario, unintimidated by the political and economic ramifications, he could. Beyond his hands-on experience with military solutions to terrorism, he possessed one other essential attribute that few others at the table could claim: the guts to speak his mind freely.

But first he took a few moments to weigh his response. Much, after all, depended on it. Hub meanwhile noticed that the general was giving the term "magnetic" an almost literal meaning. The man's charisma—the curt savvy in his eyes, the set of his mouth, the generally electric force of his persona—created a kind of gravity well. It exerted a palpable pull on the attention of all present.

At precisely the same moment General William Devereaux composes his thoughts—

During those same several seconds—

A scant moment by some measures, an eternity by others—

A ritual unfolds in an anonymous room—

Water flows over anonymous hands.

Walls of stone, the tang of steam in the air—

A solemn chanting echoes through, sonorous with faith—

Resonant of purity—

Over the hands, water flows.

Devereaux looked up, making eye contact with the people staring at him. When he spoke his voice rang authoritatively through the room. "Twelve hours after the president gives the word we can be on the ground. One light infantry division of ten thousand seven hundred men. Elements of the Rapid Deployment Force combined with Special Forces, Delta Forces. APCs, tanks, helicopters. And, of course, the ubiquitous M–16A1 assault rifle, a humble weapon until you see a man carrying one outside your local bowling alley or 7-Eleven." The library's somber atmosphere darkened further. Devereaux added, "It will be noisy, it will be scary, and it will not be mistaken for a VFW parade."

Senator Wright and Congressman Marshall exchanged veiled glances. The attorney general rubbed her nose.

In the stone-walled room—

The anonymous hands, dry now, lift a cotton shroud—

The fabric billows through the air, dappled with light reflecting from water—

Showing its fine weave—

The shroud drifts down—Down—

Over a youthful shoulder—

"That means civilian casualties," Devereaux continued. "At a minimum it's a drunk private joyriding in a Hummer who runs down an old lady in Greenpoint. At a maximum..." The general sighed, glancing away. His face tightened. "Make no mistake," he said with conviction. "We will hunt the enemy. We will find the enemy. And we will *kill* the enemy."

Devereaux sounded as if he were making an unqualified vow. In a sense, he was. But none of those listening was prepared for the sentiment he next expressed.

* * *

A key slides into an ignition lock—
    The anonymous hand turns it—
    A starter whines—
    An engine rumbles to life—

Devereaux said passionately, "And no card-carrying member of the ACLU is more dead set against it . . ." He paused for dramatic effect, looking around the room. ". . . than I am."

Huh, thought Hub. *The general is making quite a production of this.*

"Which is why I urge you!" Devereaux proclaimed. "No, I *implore* you—not to consider this option."

A bemused silence greeted the finale.

Seconds ticked by. Todd Franklin sighed, in a way pregnant with decision. He remarked, "I know what the president will say."

"What's that?" Devereaux asked.

"That's exactly why you're the only man for the job," the White House chief of staff replied.

On an anonymous street in an anonymous part of town—
    A garage door rattles open—
    Darkness within—
    Something roaring there—
    Tires squeal—
    A van hurtles forth like a beast from a cave.

* * *

Hub digested the chief of staff's statement: Devereaux, "the only man for the job." *Not my first choice,* Hub reflected, wondering.

The other general, the four-star to whom Hub couldn't put a name, spoke up. "I remind you," he said sternly, "that General Devereaux does not speak for official army policy. A police function has become accepted as our role in Haiti, in Somalia . . ."

"Could I interrupt?" Hub inquired, surprising no one more than himself.

Heads swiveled, taking in the source of the upstart voice.

16

Only two people at the library table recognized the man who had called out from the meeting's fringes. The FBI director was one. General Devereaux was the other.

Devereaux smiled. "That's Anthony Hubbard, FBI," he announced graciously. "He's the ASAC on the ground up there. They took out the first cell less than thirty-six hours after Bus 87." Interest sharpened in the eyes trained on Hub. "I suggest," Devereaux concluded, "we hear what he has to say."

Devereaux nodded at Hub, giving him the floor. Hub returned the nod, acknowledging the vote of confidence. He cleared his throat, and said, "There is something you probably haven't thought about doing."

The room's interest level notched up. Todd Franklin said, "And that is?"

"Nothing," Hub said steadily. "Don't overreact."

The interest level remained high, but only temporarily, for it now held incredulity bordering on shock. "With all respect," Hub continued, "I'm just a cop. To you these people may be martyrs, but to me they're criminals. And a criminal is no more than somebody who thinks he's better than everyone else." Hub shook his head to reinforce his next point. "And he's *not* better. He only has to be wrong once. And that's where we come in. We run down a tip from a landlord, or we pick up a latent print from a bus. Our phones are ringing off the hook with people from the Arab community wanting to help."

The FBI director studied his fingernails. *No endorsement there,* Hub thought. He rallied himself, resolving to stick to his guns. "They love this country, and they hate that these criminals are giving them a bad name," he went on, measuring his words carefully, only too aware that he had no experience conducting himself in such circumstances. "With their help and some old-fashioned shoe leather, we'll nail these guys."

"Amen to that," Devereaux intoned.

Chief of Staff Franklin said, "Thank you, Agent Hubbard. I, too, think we should proceed cautiously." He glanced around the room, measuring the reaction. Impassive faces told him little, other than the previously established fact that no one here really had a clue how to proceed. Hub's comments had merely stirred up already-muddy waters. To do nothing was politically impossible.

"Now we've got an Agency briefing prepared," Franklin plowed on, changing the subject. "Some of you may not know Sharon Bridger. Sharon was posted in Iraq as part of our covert operations during the Gulf War." His eyes reached to the back of the room. "Sharon?"

When a voice replied, Hub's head snapped up. But he didn't need to look at the source; he could tell who it was. "We all know the traditional model of a terrorist network," the voice said. "One cell controlling all others. Cut off the head, and the body will wither."

Hub turned to face the room's rear. The woman just identified as Sharon Bridger went by another name as well—Elise Kraft.

She caught Hub's stare blithely, as if nothing were amiss, and proceeded with her analysis. "Unfortunately, the old wisdom no longer applies. The new paradigm is like the myth of the Hydra. Each cell exists independently from the others. Cut off one head and another rises up in its place."

Holy shit, Hub thought. How many identities did Elise—Sharon?—maintain? She looked good in her power suit. At ease. Knowledgeable. Accustomed to enlightening people like this.

Someday Hub would ask her about multiple

identities. Right now, though, he wanted to hear her thoughts about the Hydra. What would she reveal to authorities of such stature? Something she hadn't revealed to him?

Come on, Sharon, Hub thought, willing the thought into his stare. *How do you fight something that defies decapitation?*

Sedately, below the speed limit, the van crosses the Brooklyn Bridge—

An anonymous van, almost indistinguishable from a hundred thousand others—

Something awaits it in the distance—

The glass towers of Manhattan—

"Bus 87 was the work of cell number one," Sharon Bridger continued. "Its elimination only activated the work of cell number two—the theater gala."

The van enters the canyons of the financial district—

It does not have much farther to go—

Frank Haddad and Danny Sussman exited the Federal Building's glass-fronted lobby. Then they crossed the open area somewhat grandiosely called Federal Plaza. With Hub in Washington both men had their hands full orchestrating the New Victory Theater investigation. The day had started very early. It promised to end quite late.

Fred Darius and Mike Johannson approached from the street, on their way back to the office after a session with technical experts who were analyzing fragments of the New Victory device. Frank considered stopping them to get the update. But he and Danny were running late. Another team of experts, on-site at the theater, had just found a strand of fiber that initial tests showed to be Egyptian cotton. That by itself wouldn't have required Frank and Danny's presence. But the political firestorm now raging due to the deaths and maimings of several hundred prominent citizens did mandate an appearance at the theater.

Frank and Danny crossed the street. A van passed, picking up speed. The sudden acceleration caught Frank's eye.

"And cell number three?" Chief of Staff Franklin asked Sharon Bridger. "How do we find cell number three?"

The question cranked up the tension in the Capitol library. Those not already looking at Sharon turned to accord her their full attention. Her expression slowly changed. Hub clocked it; for reasons he couldn't put his finger on, he suddenly felt sure that Sharon knew something about cell number three. That alarmed him. Partly because Sharon was taking her time in replying; if she had information, why not spit it out? Her face turned pensive. As if something startling had just crossed her mind.

Say it, Hub silently urged the woman. *Tell us what you know about cell number three.*

Rooted to the ground, Frank and Danny watched the van jump the curb. It heaved onto the sidewalk, jounced for a moment, then roared across the plaza. On a collision course with the Federal Building's glassed lobby.

At last Sharon Bridger spoke. "We don't know," she told the meeting. "We simply don't know how to find cell number three."

The shock wave blew Frank and Danny through a dry cleaner's storefront window. That saved their lives.

The Federal Building's facade rippled upward, forty-seven stories of glass transformed to mist. The debris climbed into the air above the building like a reaching hand. It rose farther, lengthening into a plume, grabbing for the sky. The plume slowed, and paused—a great cloud of smithereens so fine, it looked as if it might remain aloft indefinitely, drifting with the breeze.

But then gravity took hold. An avalanche of rubble, a great many thousands of tons of it—glass, concrete, splintered wood, wiring, the remains of furniture, of bodies—thundered into the street with the force of a pyroclastic flow.

"Thank you, Sharon," Chief of Staff Franklin said without enthusiasm. "Now then. Can we achieve a consensus to present to the president?"

Hub didn't see how that was possible. The different points of view appeared to have canceled each other out.

The four-star army general, his face stony, said, "There is precedent . . ."

He only got out those three words. *En masse*, clamorously, telephones and pagers buzzed.

17

Hub stood before what remained of the Federal Building, riven with shock. Shadows were lengthening under early-afternoon light, darkening a vast gash of rubble and ruptured floors that rose the full height of the forty-seven-story shell. Legions of rescue workers from the tristate region continued to search for survivors, bodies, and body parts. They had been at work a full four hours; hope, with regard to finding more living victims, was ebbing. With regard to the dead the operation still had a long way to go. A fleet of ambulances, parked at a distance to avoid falling debris, received a continual delivery of stretcher-borne bags. Hub had given up counting how many he'd seen carried from the ruins. But he couldn't stop attaching mental snapshots of faces.

Frank approached and stood silently alongside, respectful of the trauma Hub was experiencing.

He himself could barely suppress a bad case of the shakes.

"Are they confirmed?" Hub said almost inaudibly.

Frank nodded. "Fred, Whitney," he muttered. "We're waiting on who else."

Hub thought about young Fred Darius, his career scarcely begun. Whitney the computer technician, a whiz and also young. The many hundreds of others—FBI, INS, IRS, DEA, unsung bureaucrats in the welfare and housing and elder affairs departments. And on, and on.

Far less significant than the body count, but as a practical matter an incalculable setback, files, computer records, and in-progress paperwork were also gone, literally cast to the winds, converted to smog. As far as New York City and environs were concerned, for the indefinite future the federal government's ability to conduct business as usual had simply vanished.

Hub hadn't just lost a place more important than home, and not just colleagues who represented a kind of substitute family. He had been deprived of a way of life; he felt like a tribesman who has just discovered that in his absence, all the villages and farms burned to the ground.

A Jeep crunched at them through debris. Elise Kraft jumped out. *No,* Hub corrected himself, *make that Sharon Bridger.* "Sharon," he called out, no affection in his voice.

For a few moments they gazed at each other, the abyss separating them deeper and murkier than ever. A uniformed military man stepped from the Jeep. "This is Colonel Hardwick," Sharon informed Hub. "Army Intelligence."

"Anthony Hubbard," Hub said to the man, shaking his hand. "Average intelligence." Hardwick didn't seem to appreciate the joke. Hub studied his face; severe, calculating, it suited his name. "But 'til I hear otherwise," Hub added, dispensing with sarcasm and getting to the point, "this is still my show."

"I'm here as an advisor only," the colonel replied. "I intend to keep a low profile."

"I appreciate that, Colonel," Hub said.

"I don't mean to be insensitive," Hardwick went on, choosing his words with care and in the process conveying a lack of genuine concern. "But what, exactly, are your capabilities at this point? Your . . ." He gestured at the gutted building. "Infrastructure?"

"You're standing on our infrastructure," Hub said coldly. "Excuse me." He walked away toward the ruins, his long coat flapping in the corpse-sweetened breeze. Hardwick's self-description as a low-profile advisor didn't impress Hub. His years of service with the 82nd Airborne had taught him some things about army mind-sets. Hardwick's attitude set off alarms. "Low-profile advisors" had directed the U.S. military's early involvement in Vietnam.

Sharon stared after Hub, chagrined that he'd cut off the introduction to Hardwick. But perhaps it was just as well. How, at this point, could one find the right thing to say?

By nightfall Hub finished transforming his apartment into a temporary command post. Agents pushed furniture to the walls, creating space in which to lay out what little they'd managed to salvage from the office: charred remnants of files, soggy dossiers, some discs, records of liaisons with the Arab community in Brooklyn.

Floyd Rose hung up one of the newly installed phones. "They managed to get a partial VIN number off the van," he told Hub. "DMV says it was reported stolen the day before in . . ."

"Brooklyn," Hub said, not feeling telepathic. Of course it had been stolen in Brooklyn.

Floyd nodded, confirming Hub's guess.

Frank joined them, his face stark. "We just got confirmation on Mike," he announced. "He was with Fred in the lobby." The news came as no surprise to Frank. He'd seen Fred and Mike enter the lobby just a minute or so before the van made its own glass-splintering entrance. Despite that, Frank had been hoping that Mike might have had business in one of the basements. An errand in the mail room, the parking garage, the commissary, whatever; if he'd left the lobby quickly enough, he just might have survived.

"How many does that make it?" Hub asked.

Someone knocked on the front door before Frank could reply. One of the agents in the living room rose to answer it. Hub and Frank eyed each other. Given the number of FBI personnel still unaccounted for, a knock might bring good news. Somebody's reappearance—back from the presumed dead?

No such luck. Sharon Bridger walked in.

She scanned the improvised office space, then approached Hub. "I'm . . ." she said haltingly, ". . . very sorry. About your friends."

"Frank," Hub said stonily, as if making introductions for the first time, "this is Sharon." He turned to her, adding with exaggerated politeness, "I didn't catch the last name?"

"Bridger," she replied. "How ya doing, Frank?"

"Been better," Frank said, giving her nothing.

Sharon nodded. She took a folder from her purse, attempting to defuse the tension with business. Hebrew script labeled the folder; *a Mossad report*, Frank told himself dispiritedly. What could they be disclosing now that wouldn't have been a hell of a lot more useful a week ago? Or yesterday? "The Agency has come up with another list of probables," Sharon explained. She extracted some photographs.

Neither Hub nor Frank showed the slightest interest.

Sharon put the photos on a coffee table. None of the other agents made a move to take a look. "I think we should circulate them," Sharon went on, gamely fighting the stonewall. "Hey, this stuff may be good."

She didn't believe what she was saying, Hub knew from her manner. The material might have some tangential relevance. But nothing more. If the photos were a smoking gun or anything close, Sharon wouldn't have brought them to Hub's apartment. Hub would have been summoned to somebody else's office to see them—to a workplace in working order, most likely Colonel Hardwick's. Sharon clearly was just trying to reach out.

When Hub spoke his tone held no forgiveness. "Why was there no warning from Samir?"

"Because he didn't know anything," Sharon replied.

"Says Samir," Frank said sharply.

"Says me," Sharon insisted.

"Maybe I'll ask him," Hub remarked, glancing at Frank.

"Over my dead body," Sharon said, her voice rising.

Hub bellowed, "Over six *hundred* dead bodies!"

In fact, the full Federal Building body count

hadn't been tallied. Six hundred could have easily been a gross underestimate.

Hub and Sharon glared at each other, neither of them able to smooth over their fatigue and ravaged nerves.

"Look," Sharon snapped. "Samir's one of the good guys. Okay?"

"How the *fuck* can you be so sure?" Hub retorted, his voice raw with disbelief.

"Because he helped me recruit the network in Iraq!" Sharon yelled. "*Okay?*" The interchange was degenerating into a shouting match. Sharon strove to control her temper. "Look," she said less loudly, "can we talk about this in private?"

Hub just stared at her, wordlessly replying: *No*.

"Okay," Sharon said yet again, aware that invoking Agency security issues would get her nowhere with people whose faith in the very concept of security had just been blown sky-high. "Fine," she added. "My job over there was to go into the destabilize-Saddam Hussein-business. Printing up fake dinars, arming the Kurds . . ."

"And financing the sheik," Frank cut in. It was a hunch he'd developed. Apart from the fact that Sharon had already admitted to bed-hopping throughout the Middle East, it made sense that the CIA would assign an agent to this case who'd had prior dealings with the mastermind behind it. Still, Frank had no idea if he'd guessed right. And he certainly didn't expect Sharon to affirm the guess even if it was on target.

But Sharon nodded. "He's Iraqi," she said, a little defensively. "He was going to be our Ayatollah Khomeini . . ."

"And help bring down Saddam?" Frank said, surprised in spite of himself. The CIA almost never admitted this kind of thing. The potential for embarrassment or worse was just too high.

Yet Sharon continued to spill her beans. "I ran the network," she said. "Samir was the go-between. He risked his life for us over there." She swallowed, her eyes suddenly bright. "I owe him, big-time."

Hub listened with growing interest. So did the other agents in the apartment; they were doing their best not to call attention to that fact. Sharon needed no reminder that she was being unusually candid. And maybe even self-incriminating. "So who are they?" Hub asked. "Give me names, give me pictures. Not some history lesson."

Sharon sighed. "I can't give you pictures, because I don't know what they look like," she replied, dropping all pretense that the photos she'd brought offered anything useful. "We did everything at arm's length. I know what the names *should* be. But they're using other names."

"So you got nothing," Hub observed. He glanced accusingly at the file on the coffee table.

"I've got Samir," Sharon pointed out.

Hub took a deep breath. His temper was beginning to feel volatile. Any moment, it would veer in the wrong direction. He demanded, "Has Samir had *any* contact with them?"

"Minimal," Sharon replied, her tone evasive.

Minimal contact doesn't equal no contact, Frank reasoned. "How does he do it?" he asked.

This time Sharon shook her head. "He can't," she said. "They initiate."

"And otherwise . . . ?" Frank pressed.

"He's waiting," Sharon said simply.

Hub reached his breaking point. "He's *waiting*?" he asked, incredulity plain on his face. "What's he waiting for? More bodies?" Sharon's line of reasoning seemed to imply that the FBI should call it a day and simply wait with Samir, following his good example. Hub's voice rose again. "We got lots more pretty buildings in midtown," he said in a rush. "Maybe he's waiting to see how many they can . . ."

"*Look*," Sharon said urgently. "I *know* how you must feel . . ."

Hub roared, "*You don't know shit how I feel!*"

Sharon didn't flinch. "They'll make contact soon," she said, her tone clipped.

"How?" Hub demanded, advancing on Sharon, menace in his voice. His eyebrows rose. "Why 'soon'?"

Sharon stood her ground. Men scarier than Hub had questioned her in a manner suggesting physical threat.

Frank saw what was coming. He took a step back, clearing the way to a closed door.

Hub's question still hung in the air: *Why soon?*

But Sharon had finished with making revelations. She glared at Hub, refusing to be intimidated into saying a word more than her training and instincts deemed appropriate. Samir was too valuable. And Hub too frazzled.

Way too frazzled, more so than Sharon knew. He seized her arm, then jerked open the door Frank had moved from and violently shoved Sharon through it.

Into the bathroom. Hub slammed the door; Sharon's request for privacy had been granted, but not on terms she'd bargained for. Hub got close, too close. He said viciously, "What's the *tradecraft*, Sharon? Ironsites, visuals? *I love all that spy shit.*"

Sharon kept her mouth shut, her face defiant.

"I'm gonna haul your boy downtown," Hub said grindingly, "strap his ass to a polygraph, and ask him all about *you*. Then I'm gonna send the transcripts to a friend at the *Times* who just loves to write about the latest CIA link to some political horror show."

It wasn't an empty threat. What Sharon had just admitted—that the CIA had financed the probable key figure behind the terror wave—would make the juiciest headline material that any editor could hope to find.

Sharon kept her cool. She declared, "You burn him, you lose any chance you ever had."

"It's 'lose-lose' from here on in," Hub snapped. "Who said *that*?"

"I'm not fucking with you," Sharon retorted.

Hub exclaimed, "How can you possibly remember *who you're fucking*?"

Her hand flashed from nowhere, whacking a flat palm across his face. Without hesitation, Hub slapped her back, equally hard. The cracking sounds resounded like gunfire in the enclosed space. Sharon went for Hub's face with clawing fingers; she was good, her training apparent in the way she very nearly drew blood. But Hub was quicker. He grabbed both of her wrists, then twisted her right arm behind her back. "My friends are dead," he hissed into her teeth-bared scowl. "My life is blown to hell. I got nothing left to lose, *bitch*."

Sharon glared at him. Waiting for his fury to subside.

It didn't subside. Hub shoved her against the sink, forcing her over it. He leaned forward, pressing harder, a knee jammed between her legs, his face almost touching hers. They'd come eyeball-to-eyeball, more ferociously than either of them could have expected. The sink shuddered under the pressure. Hub pressed harder.

Sharon gasped, "I need"—she shook her head, unable now to escalate the contest of wills—"more time. Please. You're hurting me."

Hub nodded. He knew he was hurting her. He wanted to hurt her.

"*Please . . .*" Sharon gasped beseechingly.

Hub heard something beyond pain in her voice. A curious form of need. Of desire?

18

That night saw a media meltdown that dwarfed even the coverage of the Oklahoma City bombing. Analysts later determined that it constituted the single biggest news phenomenon in the history of broadcast journalism.

Several factors contributed to the furor. First, the Manhattan Federal Building's destruction brought far more fatalities than had the Oklahoma tragedy, or indeed any other terrorist attack of the recent era, including the embassy bombings in Nairobi and Dar es Salaam. Second, the crisis had been developing over a period of time; rather than arriving as a surprise out of the blue. Blue paint had launched it to maximum mediagenic effect, establishing a stage for the increasingly horrific escalations. With such a kickoff, no one could chart the ultimate outcome. No one even had a clue as to the resources and persistence of the enemy, which all by itself guaranteed a ratings boom. Media heaven: a runaway story with no end in sight. On top of that, the enemy had presented a foreign face, one easier to hate, and easier to generate morbid fascination about, than the heartland visage of Timothy McVeigh. Something else kindled the firestorm as well. The attacks weren't killing folks in a dusty backwater state or dusty African countries. They were killing citizens and celebrities and law-enforcement personnel in glittering New York City—the very epicenter of media, the media capital of the world.

But the paramount reason TV sets everywhere were playing overtime had to do with yet another difference from earlier terrorist incidents. New York's entire population starred in this show—and not simply because they were dealing with grief. They were dealing with fear. With downright, ongoing terror. Evidence for this presented itself throughout the metropolitan area. Nothing remained normal. On any given street news cams could capture that most riveting of spectacles: Americans succumbing to panic.

The *Fox News Special Report* led with the following headline:

NEW YORK UNDER SIEGE

"Tonight we take a close look at the tragic sight of a city under siege." Variations of that sentence opened reports from newsrooms worldwide, providing a context for images that billions of viewers could

not resist no matter where they sat—whether it was London, Tokyo, Moscow, or Pretoria, location played no role. Ratings skyrocketed.

Despite the disaster-flick craze that had made a specialty of leveling New York, few people had ever expected to see an eerie real-life version of the same thing. A deserted Times Square, its gaudy neon playing to no one but cops. Police checking packages outside department stores, roughly detaining anyone who dared to protest. Long lines filing through checkpoints at bus stops, where buses were summarily converted to transport for the swelling number of prisoners. No laughter, no joy, no madcap nightlife in the city that couldn't sleep.

New York suddenly seemed like Stalingrad, circa 1955.

By the next morning partial normality had returned. Although many people weren't going to work or had fled the city, a large number of others couldn't afford those options. Traffic surged through the avenues and streets.

Hub and Sharon met by prearrangement at a downtown intersection. After the previous night's bathroom brawl, neither one cared to rendezvous at Hub's apartment. Nor were they eager to share a meal, or even a cup of coffee. The Federal Building office no longer remained an option. That left the pavement outside.

They walked along in silence a minute or two, absorbing obvious and not-so-obvious signs that the city was under siege. Passersby looked wanly apprehensive, skittish in their gaits, as if prepared to flee at the slightest sign of trouble. The stress didn't seem to worsen New York's legendarily rude sidewalk behavior. Somewhat the contrary; bumps and jostles tended to elicit apologetic mutters instead of insults. People were holding their breath, anxious to stay at peace. The great majority had zero desire to rock the boat.

But a minority felt otherwise. A radio newscaster blared from a passing cab: "—thus far claiming responsibility for the bombing. In other news, a cab driver was beaten and his cab set on fire. The driver, Rashid Abu . . ."

Hub recalled the Arab taxi driver who'd refused to pick him up a couple of nights before. Abdul Hassam, the ID placard had said. How was Abdul dealing with the mounting xenophobia?

Talk radio emanated from another car: "The Jews, man. When they say, 'Jump!,' we say, 'How high?' I say we . . ."

The strident voice was lost in a squeal of brakes. Hub wondered how long things like sidewalk civility could last. Was the city headed for sectarian strife? Wholesale riots in Crown Heights, Park Slope?

He and Sharon stopped at an intersection, waiting for the light to change. A bus idled before them. Cops stood conspicuously behind the driver. All buses now were considered potential neighborhood-smashing bombs, and received armed protection. Would that do any good?

Hub had no idea but was glad to see the cops anyway. Sharon turned to him, catching his eye, signaling her readiness to talk. "Samir says he can try to set up a meet by tomorrow night," she confided. "He knows they need money."

Hub nodded. He put off for the time being the question Sharon had to be expecting: How does Samir know that?

Sharon's voice dropped. "First he leaves a visual signal on his . . ."

A loud *bang* erased her voice. Pedestrians screamed and dropped to the pavement; people flinched the length of the block, then ducked into doorways. Cars hit their brakes. A bicycle messenger wiped out on the turn he was making.

But it was just the bus. Backfiring.

Hub and Sharon watched pedestrians get a grip on the false alarm. Nervous laughter rang out. The fallen picked themselves up and hurried away. A trio of teenagers doubled over with laughter; nudging each other, they pointed out the more awkward recoveries. In the minds of some this classified as comedy.

Hub didn't get the laughs. Loud bangs did nothing for his tinnitus. That sound hummed in his ears: white noise from hell, the afterglow of Bus 87. He swallowed, willing the pressure away. His ears tingled; he dreaded a full-fledged onset of roaring deafness.

But the sound dissipated. Hub took a deep breath, then headed out across the street. He asked Sharon over his shoulder, "He leaves a signal? On what?"

As the day advanced, the TV coverage became grimmer. If at first a gallows sense of humor and camaraderie had helped residents cope with the crisis, by late morning it was clear that things were getting progressively more ugly. A newscaster warned in a live report, "While many flee, others are staying behind to pay the price."

Many of the fleeing also paid a price. Every freeway out of the city was jammed, moving along on a stop-and-go basis for the lucky, frozen solid for others. Accidents compounded the congestion as the city's me-first attitude resurfaced and drivers cut dangerous corners. Midtown intermittently knotted into gridlock. It seemed that anyone with access to a car was determined to use it.

The situation hindered emergency vehicles, which only made the situation worse as ambulances, fire trucks, and cop cars resorted to sirens and brute force to maintain mobility. Fights broke out over infractions imagined and real; summary arrests were made. Abandoned cars became a serious problem, accumulating on sidewalks, then in the streets, adding to the sclerosis faster than tow trucks could clear it away.

The noontime news brought chilling images of looted delicatessens in Brooklyn. Mobs had savaged the Arab owners; bloodied faces stared condemningly from TV screens, asking what they had done to deserve such punishment.

And in a development that prompted more citizens to pack bags and get out, the police department announced new security measures for the city's public schools. Henceforth all students would be thoroughly searched before being allowed to enter. Video accompanying the story illustrated the policy's implementation: elementary-school kids surrendering backpacks to impatient officers.

Anger and fear were reaching a critical mass. Hub consulted with the mayor's office. He and a senior administrative assistant agreed that something had to be done about the city's overall approach. They scheduled an emergency early-afternoon meeting of relevant officials—police, the district attorney, community representatives—at a midtown theater.

TV news trucks were waiting out front when Hub arrived. He paused to answer a reporter's question about interdepartmental coordination. Nearby another reporter told a camera, "Today, as hundreds of law-enforcement officials gather in a Broadway theater, people outside want answers. How far can the crackdown go? How many more extreme measures? Already there is talk of a protest march by a coalition of . . ."

Hub had heard enough. At this point, protest marches scarcely could stop the city's drift toward flash point. He excused himself from further questions and moved through the security line into the theater's lobby.

The auditorium's orchestra seats were filled with representatives of various law-enforcement departments. Hub took a chair on the stage, joining a handful of senior administrators. He was disappointed to note the rancorous exchange under way. The mayor's assistant wasn't contributing to the "calm dialogue" he'd called for earlier on the phone. He bellowed at Danny Sussman, "The *people* of this *city* have a *right* . . . !"

Danny occupied a particularly sensitive position as the liaison between the NYPD and the Terrorism Task Force. He cut off the mayoral AA with his own raised voice: "The *purpose* of this *meeting* is to—"

"*Is to make the city safe!*" the AA shouted, his face alarmingly red. "And your *department* . . ."

Danny exploded. "My department *what, asshole?*"

Hub scanned the crowd sitting below him. At the rear he glimpsed Sharon Bridger. Discreetly, she waved.

The district attorney raised his arm. "Guys, guys," he said reprovingly.

But then a dozen or so loud voices joined the fray, generating pandemonium.

Hub grabbed a microphone and slapped a hand over it. Feedback reverb squealed through the cavernous space. The sound delivered the impact Hub wanted. The cacophony quieted.

"Sorry," Hub told the crowd with an authoritative smile. "From now on, we will raise our hands and wait to be *called on*."

Appreciative chuckles greeted the edict; the cooler heads present welcomed Hub's headmasterly approach. He pointed at a man in a dark suit who had raised his hand.

"Howard Kaplan, INS," the man said, rising to his feet. He glanced around, seeking faces he recognized. "So we've pulled every ethnic visa in the city and traced them to source," he announced. "Who wants 'em?"

Hub turned to Danny Sussman. "Danny?"

Sussman shrugged. "We bring 'em in, have a talk," he replied. His manner implied it wouldn't be a problem.

A uniformed cop stood in the orchestra. "What about translators?" he asked.

The district attorney leaned forward with a skeptical frown. "How many people we talking about here?"

"Sixteen hundred, maybe more," Kaplan from INS said.

Danny stiffened. "Where the hell we gonna put sixteen hundred people?" he demanded.

The question reignited a competing babble of voices. Hub got to his feet and took control. He singled out someone raising his hand in the orchestra.

"What about a military presence at JFK and La Guardia?" the man suggested.

"I don't think we're there yet," Hub replied. He waved dissenters to silence. "It's also not going to stop these people."

The mayor's man said, "What about protecting the Arab population? There's a lot of anger—"

A dignified gentleman rose. He declared, "I represent the American-Arab Anti-Discrimination Committee. Whatever injustices my people may be suffering at this difficult moment, we will continue to show our patriotism and our commitment to this country."

The statement fell on receptive ears. At the same time, a stir passed through the room. Everyone knew that the most explosive political issue before them concerned the rights of the Arab community.

"Thank you, sir," Hub said gratefully. "And to

everyone else for their patience today. These are extremely difficult times—London, Paris, we're not the first city to have to deal with this."

The Arab community representative nodded. He retook his seat.

Hub considered what these people really needed to hear. "In Tel Aviv," he remarked, "the day after they blew up the market, the market was full." He let that sink in, making eye contact with anxious faces in the audience. "This is New York," he said rousingly. "We can take it!"

Dozens nodded in agreement. Hub breathed an inward sigh of relief. The meeting seemed to be approaching a consensus that, no matter how bad things got, somehow they would ride it out. That was the critical first step, in Hub's view. Without determination and unity the best intentions would come to naught . . .

Two hundred beepers and phones suddenly buzzed throughout the theater.

The sound broke the spell Hub was trying to cast. Everyone looked around, wondering: *Dear God, what now?*

19

The street was thick with cop cars when Hub arrived on the scene, and antiriot personnel were keeping onlookers at bay. Sharon somehow had managed to insert herself into Hub's car during the fracas outside the theater following the breakup of the meeting. She accompanied him as he passed through the police line and entered the latest hot zone in the city's ordeal.

The place made Hub's skin crawl. He and others had feared that the terrorists would choose just this kind of target: an elementary school.

A sergeant escorted them through halls decorated with exuberant finger-painted murals, productions at which the resident artists excelled, then up a flight of stairs. In a second-floor corridor lay the first signs of trouble. Desks and tables had been upended to form a makeshift blast barricade. Cops, Hub's senior FBI team, and a police technician huddled behind it, staring at a surveillance monitor. As Hub approached, the technician adjusted a control board. The image on the monitor shifted slightly. The technician had managed to deploy a mobile camera.

Hub noted the cable snaking down the corridor. It passed under a closed door. He knelt behind the barricade to get a look at the monitor. Sharon, his shadow, knelt beside him.

The monitor told a fuller story. Its grainy black-and-white image indicated that the technician was using an "arthroscopic" camera probe. Small children huddled in a corner of the classroom behind the closed door, clutching each other, bawling with fright. A woman lay on the floor, dark wet surrounding her, dead. A pair of legs was visible to one side. Hub surmised that they belonged to a terrorist.

Danny Sussman and Frank Haddad had arrived two minutes before. Danny explained to Hub, "One of the moms was carrying a piece, wounds the guy as he's planting the device. He kills her and locks them all in." Danny gestured at the screen. "Up there in the corner. By the clock."

Hub studied the wall-mounted bomb. It looked like a smaller version of the Semtex jobs that the terrorists had been using. If it blew, no one in the room stood a chance. Hell, the people in the corridor counting on the desk barricade for protection were taking a sizable gamble.

"It's got a timer on it," Danny continued. "Only we don't know how much time is left."

Hub stared at the horrifying image. Something in his head dislodged. His sinuses seemed to heat up. Then he heard it—the sound he dreaded, the more so because only he could hear it. The white noise that blossomed into unbearable pain.

"Closer on the timer," Hub ordered. He tried to banish the noise from his head. It only grew louder.

"I'm trying," the technician said. "But the angle's wrong . . ."

Something making a great deal of noise approached the exterior of the building. In Hub's head it merged with white noise, increasing the pressure on his ears. He glanced through an open doorway at the far wall of a classroom. It held large plate-glass windows. Hub stared, at first unable to comprehend what was heaving into view beyond the windows: an NYPD SWAT helicopter, a marksman in position at an open door. The chopper hovered, clearly angling for a line of fire on the building. On the windows of the classroom down the corridor.

Frank yelled, "What the fuck is the NYPD doing here?"

Danny looked worried. "I don't know," he said. "Somebody must have . . ."

Frank screamed, *"We've run drills on this jurisdiction bullshit since—"*

Danny whirled to him. *"I know!"* he shouted. "You think *I* . . ."

"Quit bickering and fix it!" Hub hollered, pain shimmering through his head like radioactive aurora borealis. He tried to focus on the helicopter. One of the marksmen was aiming his rifle. He looked to be drawing a bead . . .

Hub's head seemed to explode. White noise cranked to a scream—unimaginably more loud, unimaginably more pure.

Danny Sussman was shouting into his radio, "NYPD SWAT, *this is the FBI. Get that bird the fuck out of there!"*

Hub didn't hear most of what Danny said. The chopper drowned him out, then the white noise pushed through, shutting everything out. It milkened the very air, and even the monitor, on which Hub now saw small children writhing with wide-open mouths—mouths that emitted not screams, but more white noise. The noise both drowned out everything and emanated from everything all at once, unifying the scene, drawing Hub's mind to a terrible point. As if with telescopic vision he saw the marksman in the chopper tighten his finger on the trigger. Hub checked the monitor again, his heart pounding. The terrorist had seized a child. He was using her as a human shield.

The noise climbed to a plateau, taking Hub farther than he'd gone before; it obliterated even the sound of the chopper. He closed his eyes. In his whited-out mind he envisioned the nightmare that was about to unfold.

He couldn't tolerate it.

And suddenly he found himself on his feet, rushing down the corridor, hurtling through a tunnel of noise toward a coruscating point of light—the closed door.

He crashed into the door and through it, wood buckling, splinters flying. Hub didn't feel the impact. The noise now enveloped him like a force field, hardening his senses even as he saw everything with preternatural clarity: the terrorist turning toward him, a hand rising with a gun, the limp girl clutched; the furious vortex of the chopper hovering beyond the windows, the marksman's rifle taking aim; the children cowering in the corner, covering little faces with little hands; the Semtex pack taped to the wall by the clock, its timer ticking, counting down. The terrorist's gun continuing to rise, swinging into position. In a fraction of a second it would spit fire . . .

Hub fired twice. Both bullets smacked into the terrorist. The man sagged. He released the child, who drifted in slow motion toward the floor. Hub didn't hear the dying terrorist shout: *"Allah Akbar!"* But he saw the words emerge from contorted lips.

The white noise crescendoed—

And then the bomb blew.

Hub was still moving. He altered his trajectory, aiming for the huddled kids. He would die. But just maybe, with his body covering them, the kids might live . . .

The shock wave thundered through the room. Warm viscosity then flooded, a blanket of unspeakable wet . . .

Agents pounded in, Sharon on their heels.

Something shiny coated much of the room. Blue paint.

Hub trembled on top of the pile of children. It took several long seconds for reality to penetrate his mind.

The chopper swung away from the windows.

I'm not dead, Hub told himself. And the children weren't dead. They weren't even injured; like the passengers of Bus 99, they had been assaulted with nothing more than paint. He drew weeping children within his arms, seeking to comfort them. To let them know that everything was finally okay.

But within Hub, everything wasn't okay. He felt his facade crack. He couldn't keep it up, his tough-guy persona, not one second more; he wept. Tears poured from his eyes, tears for the victims of the bombings, for the children here who had escaped death, and tears for himself, too. For the man who was supposed to be making all of this go away.

Agents, cops, the technician, and Sharon stood around, taking in the scene. It stilled them. For a moment they were unable to react. They felt vaguely embarrassed. As if they'd burst without permission into an intimate moment.

In fact, it was Hub's emotion that stilled them. They were more than a little moved.

20

That night Hub sprawled on the sofa in his living room, watching CNN's account of the elementary-school attack. He'd stripped to his boxers, ridding himself of paint-soaked clothes; with a towel he tried to remove paint from his hair. At least it was latex. Not an oil-base that only kerosene would dissolve.

The thought made him smile. Not broadly; dull shrieks still patrolled his brain, ghosts of white noise. Still, he smiled, his first of the day. He'd been damn lucky, luckier than when the claymore hadn't blown. Compared to Semtex, blue paint amounted to a kiss. He could have dealt with kerosene.

The CNN story made much of his heroism. It lamented the murder of the gun-wielding mother, warned that such moms sometimes aren't a good idea no matter how valiant they might be, played down the near disaster that the NYPD chopper had brought, and reported at length on the trauma suffered by the children and their parents. Hub listened as his mind strayed elsewhere: to Brooklyn, its ethnic enclaves. To unknown people plotting their next move.

But CNN's closing segment captured his full attention. It raised some questions that he himself had been thinking over at length.

Why had the terrorists reverted to the tactic they'd used in their opening salvo? After the serial carnage of Bus 87, the New Victory Theater, and the Federal Building, why a reprise of harmless blue paint?

The enemy had sacrificed a man in the classroom but had deliberately chosen not to kill most of the victims there. A gesture of mercy? What kind of mercy? And why?

Hub thought he knew the answer. So did CNN. The Special Report featured analysts who told of rumors that the terrorists had a specific objective in mind. Unlike the World Trade Center and embassy bombers, simple rage didn't fuel them; they weren't trying to exact revenge for a broad range of grievances. Instead, they apparently were seeking the release of a leader who they believed to be in covert U.S. military custody. Thus the blue paint: Might it signify not mercy, but a warning that unless their demand was met, the carnage would resume with even greater savagery? In view of what had followed the first paint attack, the possibility had to be taken seriously.

The CNN analysts wouldn't hazard a guess as to who the captured leader might be. However, they referred to him as "a sheik."

Hub brooded about Ahmed bin Talal. Dead? Alive? Who was telling the truth? Although he had no idea how to find out, he concurred with CNN on one thing. The terrorists wouldn't stop until they either were destroyed or got what they wanted. There lay the real import of the blue paint.

A soft knock sounded on the front door. Hub grabbed a pair of pants and pulled them on. When he opened the door it was Sharon in the hall. She looked concerned.

"You all right?" she asked.

Hub nodded.

Sharon held a piece of paper. "This just came in," she said, handing it to him.

Another fax, Hub saw. The message read:

LAST WARNING. RELEASE HIM.

Hub stood aside, opting for body language over words to invite Sharon in. She took off her coat. Almost casually, she asked, "You still believe Devereaux?"

Hub never had known whether or not to believe the general's story on bin Talal's fate. He didn't trust Devereaux. The man's bravado, and his undisguised contempt for the president, struck Hub as unprofessional. He sensed that Devereaux's penchant for immaculate suits camouflaged a rogue interior. And, quite possibly, a liar.

Sharon watched Hub close the door. Hub felt her eyes on him; felt them checking out his bare torso. She said, "Samir says the meet is on for tomorrow. Have you got enough manpower for the stakeout?"

Hub nodded. "I'll get it," he said. With a gesture he urged Sharon to take a seat.

Hours later, exhausted from combing through analyses of the incident at the school, Hub and Sharon relaxed on the sofa, files and documents strewn before them. Sharon sat with her feet drawn under her rear end; her shoes, long since removed, lay on the floor. She and Hub were each nursing a second scotch on the rocks.

Hub tossed a file onto the coffee table. In a puzzled tone he declared, "If you're on the State Department Terrorist Watch List, you *cannot* get into this country. But these two . . ." He gestured at the file; it contained dossiers on a couple of the dead terrorists. "*Both* of them were on the Watch List. And they got in."

"Did you call the State Department?" Sharon asked.

"They told me to call INS," Hub replied.

"And?" Sharon inquired.

"INS told me to call State," Hub said disgustedly.

"Don't you just love government?" Sharon asked with a smile.

Hub rolled his head over his shoulders, trying to stretch out tension in his neck.

Sharon watched sympathetically. "Bad?"

Hub raised his drink, and said, "This helps."

"That was a pretty crazy thing you did today," Sharon remarked. "Pretty brave, too."

Hub was tired of hearing about his bravery. At the time, deafened by white noise, running head-long down a corridor he was sure would explode, he hadn't really even known what he was doing. Again he rolled his head.

"Here," Sharon said, moving closer, offering to rub his neck. Her fingers sank in and found corded muscles. Expertly, she kneaded them.

Hub grunted, grateful for the combination of pain, release, and relief. "Where'd you learn how to do that?" he asked.

"Trade secret," Sharon murmured.

Hub closed his eyes. "Samir like it?"

The question didn't seem to bother Sharon; her fingers continued to knead steadily. "Look," she said, "I'm a girl. I use what I've got. I do what I have to do. Running an agent can have all sorts of distasteful requirements, or fringe benefits—depending on how you look at it."

That's commitment for you, Hub thought. "How about running an FBI agent?" he asked.

Sharon snorted. "You think I'm trying to run you?"

Hub turned to look at her. "What exactly do you call this?" he asked sharply.

Sharon met his stare and returned it. "What does it feel like?" she said.

It happened to feel quite wonderful, but that answered Sharon's question, not Hub's. The mutual stare lengthened; in each other's eyes they discerned something removed from the bombings, from spycraft, from the issue of who was running whom. An underlying truth emerged, plainer, more simple: They were both sad and lonely people, with no time for lives beyond the nightmare consuming the city.

"You want me to stop?" Sharon asked.

Hub took her hand from his neck, then held it. "You want me to start?" he asked.

They gazed into each other a few moments more. Then they moved closer and embraced, unlocking a passion that each had suppressed through the harrowing ups and downs of the previous few days. Negative emotions had defined their relationship; paradoxically, they now contributed to mutual attraction. That reality surfaced in the ferocity, the desperate neediness, of their first kiss.

They proceeded into serious sex, both finding something more than comfort, a whole lot less than love.

Todd Franklin was working late in his spacious East Wing office at the White House. His wife, Minnie, at home with the kids, was not happy about that state of affairs. Despite the fact that she'd had plenty of time to get used to it.

What did she expect? Franklin wondered. That running the White House for a president in crisis meant loads of time for squalling brats?

At the moment he had his hands full with a very different kind of brat. Franklin keyed the intercom. "Send him in," he told the secretary in the outer office.

General William Devereaux strode through the door, as usual looking like a million bucks in an impeccable suit. Franklin sat back, both amused and a little uneasy. Devereaux's sartorial close-order drill could be seen as just another manifestation of the man's much-noted discipline. On the other hand, it could reflect something else. Narcissism, for example. Franklin's job exposed him on a daily basis to powerful individuals. Experience had taught him that these people could be grouped into two different categories. Those who drew on inner security to further their ambitions. And those who drew on insecurity.

Devereaux, of course, appeared to be an exemplar of self-possessed drive and charm. Then again, so did most of the people with whom Franklin dealt. The differences between the two categories almost always lay below the surface. Franklin hadn't yet made up his mind about Devereaux. But he harbored doubts.

"The FBI received another fax," he told the general.

"Ahmed bin Talal," Devereaux replied, smartly erect. "They're still under the impression that we have him."

"Do we?" Franklin asked. "Have him?"

Devereaux sighed. "To refresh your memory, as I told you last time, it was the Libyans who . . ."

"I remember perfectly well what you told me last time," Franklin interrupted. He leaned forward, looking Devereaux in the eye. "Do we?"

Devereaux's face frosted. "Let me give you some free advice, son," he said with a condescension that few visitors to this office dared to show. "Don't get between me and the president. You might break a nail."

Franklin replied smoothly, "I am speaking for the president."

The two men measured each other, weighing the fact that the conversation actually concerned only one topic: plausible deniability.

Devereaux said, "As far as the president is concerned . . ." Unfinished sentences weren't part of the general's verbal repertoire. Unless they served a purpose. "No," he then said. "We do not."

Franklin nodded, accepting the answer, knowing what it meant. Of course Devereaux was holding the sheik. That didn't really matter. For the time being, at least, Franklin could deal with it. More urgent matters required his attention. He said, "General, do you know that after yesterday's attack, half the parents in this country kept their children out of school?"

Devereaux nodded, a glint in his eyes. Every idiot knew that people were keeping their kids at home.

"They're attacking our way of life," Franklin went on. "And the president cannot afford to be made to appear weak."

Devereaux's eyebrows rose. Franklin was saying something in his own kind of code, one as transparent as the general's. "Are you saying the president is prepared to take the necessary steps?" he asked

"I'm saying," Franklin replied, "that the president is prepared to be—presidential."

Devereaux nodded. The order had been given.

21

Hub woke at dawn, his dream shattered by the ringing phone. Bedsheets entangled him in alien ways; he sat up and looked around, for a moment unable to recall the events of the night before. Then he saw that he was alone, and remembered. Or did he? Had he really slept with Sharon?

He reached for the phone. "Hubbard," he mumbled.

The excited voice on the line made no sense.

"*What?*" Hub barked. "Slow down, slow down . . ."

It was Danny Sussman, full of information about the army making a move in Brooklyn. Only one coherent idea stood out in the NYPD liaison's rapid recitation of facts. The development was playing big on early-edition TV news.

Hub decided to go to the source. He reached for his remote control.

The image that came on instantly clarified his mind. Caterpillar treads were grinding across pavement under dawn's gray light: the treads of the lead armored personnel carrier of a long column of military vehicles, advancing over the Brooklyn Bridge.

Holy fuck, Hub thought. It looked like the real thing—a full-fledged army invasion of Brooklyn. Only one person could have authorized this. Why the hell hadn't Hub been informed? How come he was getting clued in from the *news*?

General Devereaux came on, his face a portrait of martial resolve. His clothing echoed his expression; no suit on the general this morning. He wore battle fatigues.

He announced grimly, "Today, with the invocation of the War Powers Act by the president, I am declaring a state of martial law in this city." The general's voice reached from the TV set like an iron claw.

Hub realized that Danny had alerted him just in time to catch Devereaux's first official announcement. He jumped out of bed, cranked the TV set's volume to near-maximum, then bolted to the bathroom and turned on the shower. He turned on the radio, to which he listened while shaving; Devereaux's voice emanated from it as well. Hub shook his head, unable to believe that both media were reporting something this monumental before he'd had the slightest inkling of it. The arrangement stank of setup. He'd been completely blindsided.

As word spread, people all over the city groggily turned on TVs. What they saw announced the beginning of a new era in municipal crisis management: Roadblocks had been established at key intersections. Armed soldiers cruised streets in Jeeps, randomly stopping and frisking motorists, particularly those whose skin color suggested Arab descent. Young soldiers patrolled on foot, staring down gang kids of the same age and background; not a difficult task when carrying assault rifles, but eerie to behold on live TV.

Devereaux's speech provided a narrative thread, one that news producers were forced to carry by default, given that the talking heads were still sipping their first cups of coffee. "To the best of our knowledge," the general told the city and the nation, "we are opposed by no more than twenty of the enemy. They are hiding among a population of roughly two million."

The Brooklyn Bridge remained open only to military traffic and carefully screened vehicles. Soldiers festooned with full battle regalia stopped cars en route to it; at gunpoint, people were forced to submit to checks of their trunks, handbags, briefcases, and IDs. Backed-up cars stretched into the gray distance as far as the eye could see, honking angrily. And helplessly.

Devereaux continued, his voice betraying no qualms about the televised rights violations: "Intelligence tells us the enemy is most likely Arab-speaking, between the ages of fourteen and thirty. That narrows our target to fifteen thousand suspects." As he spoke a news cam zoomed to a scuffle on one of the bridge's access roads: A sergeant dragged a swarthy youth from a car. The kid resisted, only to be summarily quelled. He was marched up the road toward the bridge, on which a number of large olive-drab tents had been erected. "We can further reduce that number," Devereaux went on, "down to those who have been in this country less than six months. Now you have twenty hiding among two thousand."

If the kid just dragged from the car were among those twenty, he would be hiding no longer. The camera tracked him and his captors as they approached one of the tents on the bridge. The boy was shoved inside, neatly illustrating Devereaux's next point: "If you are one of these twenty young men, you can hide among a population of similar ethnic background. Unfortunately for you, you can *only* hide there. And that population, in the classic immigration pattern, is concentrated. Right here in Brooklyn."

Hub's taxi dropped him off a couple of blocks

from the Manhattan side of the bridge. He sprinted through automotive chaos, scanning the crowd for Sharon. He glimpsed a redhead; she stood near the access ramp, listening to Devereaux's voice relaying from every car radio within earshot:

"We intend to seal off this borough. And then we intend to squeeze it. This is the land of opportunity, gentlemen. The opportunity to turn yourselves in. After sundown tonight any young man fitting the profile I described who has not cooperated will be arrested and detained."

Hub approached Sharon and touched her arm. She turned to him, looking pale. Like Hub, she hadn't expected the thoroughness of the operation, the overwhelming Orwellian scale. They hurried to the checkpoint barricading the bridge. An MP asked for IDs. He glanced at their badges, and said, "Would you follow me, please. The general is expecting you."

Devereaux's voice continued to echo from cars and trucks: "There is historically nothing more corrosive to the morale of an army than policing its own citizens."

The MP led Hub and Sharon up onto the bridge, then to the tent where the Arab youth had been taken. Inside, Colonel Hardwick was interrogating the boy. Devereaux sat at a desk in the rear, speaking into a microphone. "But the enemy would be sadly mistaken," the general was saying, "if they were to doubt our resolve. They are now face-to-face with the most fearsome killing machine in the history of man. And I intend to use it. And be back on base in time *for the playoffs*. That is all."

Devereaux caught sight of Hub. He rose and strode to him. "Hub," he said energetically. "Good to see you again."

"I can't say the same, sir," Hub replied, staring at Devereaux's fatigues. "Not in that uniform. I thought you were against this."

"It's past that, Hub," Devereaux said. "You're down three touchdowns. Time to bring in the first string."

"Against our own team?" Hub asked indignantly. "You run tanks down the streets of an American city and . . ."

Devereaux stiffened. "Are you questioning my patriotism?" he demanded.

Hub refused to be cowed. He declared, "I'm questioning your judgment, yes, sir."

"Hub," Devereaux snapped, his voice steel-edged, "I want you to take a moment and reflect on my life as a soldier. I have a dozen tropical diseases I'll never entirely get rid of. I set off metal detectors with the shrapnel in my ass. I have watched men die, and I have killed. Now I am serving my president and quite possibly *not* the best interests of my country, but my profession doesn't afford me the luxury of that distinction. I won't question *your* patriotism, but don't you ever again question my command."

"I'm not *under* your command, General," Hub said through clenched teeth.

Devereaux boomed, "Take a good look around, my friend, and tell me that's still true."

Just slightly, Hub's shoulders sagged.

Devereaux's face defrosted. He said in a more reasonable tone, "But we're not shutting you out. In fact, I can't do business without you, Hub. I need men like you. Men willing to put it on the line like you did in that schoolroom." He jerked a finger at his uniform, at the stars on his shoulders. "These stars mean I have been putting it on the line for thirty years—and never made a mistake worth remembering. Don't tell me I've made a mistake about you."

Hub stared into Devereaux's flinty eyes. What did the man mean about making a mistake? What did he expect Hub to do?

The general didn't elaborate. Hub stiffly took his leave. Sharon followed him out of the tent without having said a word.

They walked down the bridge, more appalled than ever by the leviathan headquartered on it. "They're not shutting me out," Hub remarked, his voice bitter with irony. "They *need* men like me."

Sharon said heatedly, "He'll fuck it up, the arrogant little prick. You ever met anybody so in love with the sound of his own voice?"

In fact, Hub was quite worried about Devereaux's seeming megalomania. It cast a question into even sharper relief: What plans did the general have for the FBI? Did he intend to use Hub's team for extralegal martial law enforcement? If so, how could Hub fight that?

But there was another, more immediate problem that he and Sharon had to confront. "What about Samir's meet?" Hub asked.

"Now?" Sharon retorted. "With all *this* going on? He's *freaked*."

"Oh, right, he's high-strung," Hub shot back. "Only you can manage him. You and the CIA and the DIA and God knows who else you're really working for!" Hub couldn't contain his frustration; he was seething. "Get back in there, Sharon, Elise, whatever the fuck your name is. They'll probably make you a colonel!"

Sharon gestured at the military might on the bridge, in the roadways and service areas beyond. "All that is no more in our interests than it is in yours, Hub."

Hub said angrily, "What, exactly, are your *interests*, Sharon? You protect Samir, you protect the Agency. You're interested in protecting everything *but* your country."

"You have no idea what I do for my country," Sharon said quietly.

"No, and I don't want to know," Hub declared.

"But the army can't do this; they'll only make it worse, and you know it." He glanced at her. "We put Samir in play. Now."

Sharon stopped walking. On her face, contrary impulses warred. She said reluctantly, "One more lamb to the slaughter."

Hub studied her. At last, Sharon seemed prepared to get real.

22

Hub and Sharon had talked things through by the time they arrived at Samir's apartment building. They'd even agreed on how to proceed.

Samir opened his door partway. He looked out, saw Hub next to Sharon. His face went ashen. The door slammed back to its frame.

But not before Hub had wedged a foot in. He forced it open. Samir, moving with frantic haste, snatched a fat joint from an ashtray and scurried to the bathroom.

Hub listened to the toilet flush. "Does he know the difference between the FBI and the DEA?" he asked Sharon.

"Samir!" Sharon called. "It's fine, he's cool."

Gunfire echoed from the streets below. Samir reappeared, wild-eyed with panic. "Listen to that!" he exclaimed. "Are you *listening*? They're killing Arabs out there!"

Hub said flatly, "You can stop it all right now."

Samir didn't understand what Hub was getting at. Or if he did, he put on a good show of pretending he didn't. Hub had a hunch that Samir was the key to finding the remaining terrorist cells. His cooperation just might wrap up the entire crisis. Maybe he really could stop it all.

But Samir didn't want to play ball. "What are you talking about?" he asked, his voice feverish. "The army is here! They're setting up interrogation centers right now! They're torturing people in cellars!"

Hub recalled "Elise's" basement den; Samir's allegation wasn't entirely without truth. And, in fact, Hub wasn't so sure that Devereaux wouldn't resort to such tactics. He said, "Let's just calm down for a second."

"I've got to get out of here," Samir stammered. "You *have to help me . . .*" He darted to a window and peered through drawn curtains.

Hub crossed to him, and said soothingly, as if gentling a horse, "We'll take care of you. Don't worry. You just have to calm down."

"Money," Samir blurted, whirling from the window. Hub studied his glassy eyes. "I must have more money!"

Sharon approached, her face hard, her eyes bright.

"You got a student visa for Ali Waziri," Hub

continued in his gentle, nonconfrontational tone. "Because . . . ?" Hub's eyebrows rose, inviting a reply. "Somebody asked you to? Didn't they, Samir?"

Samir said, "I . . ." He swallowed, then nervously wiped his mouth. "I got it myself," he volunteered.

Sharon's hand flashed out, cracking Samir across the mouth. "*Liar!*" she shouted brutally.

Samir stared at her, astonished and newly afraid. He ran his tongue around his teeth, feeling something. *Blood*, Hub thought. *Samir's turn to taste that bitter sting.*

Sharon got in Samir's face, and snarled, "You—tell him—what he wants to know."

Hub turned to Sharon, his manner offended, as if her behavior shocked him. "Hey, that's enough," he said reprovingly.

"He knows," Sharon growled. "He fucking *knows.*"

"She's crazy," Samir mumbled, his voice uneven now, cracking, his eyes glassier. "They're ghosts! *Jinn.* They'd *never* trust someone like me!"

"Stop simpering," Sharon commanded.

"Please . . ." Samir implored her.

Sharon said in the most menacing tone that Hub had heard her use to date, "I've got a picture of the two of us, do you remember that picture, Samir?" Psychic layers peeled from her face, removing a mask, exposing the ruthlessness she generally kept veiled from view, especially from Samir. Her eyes fixed on him with the calculation of an owl selecting a rodent for dinner. "I'm going to post that picture in every mosque in Brooklyn," Sharon continued. "And then I'm gonna send copies to some friends of mine on the West Bank." Samir blanched. "You've got family there, don't you?" Sharon inquired coldly.

Samir seemed to have trouble breathing.

Hub seized Sharon by the arm. "Let go of me!" she yelled.

But Hub gave her the bum's rush to the door and out the apartment. He closed the door. Then, moving deliberately, suggesting he had no ugly surprises in store, he turned back to Samir.

Samir sat still, looking utterly aghast.

"Now," Hub said, coming closer. "Nobody's going to burn you, nobody's going to call anybody." He took a seat beside Samir. "Who asked you to get that visa?"

Samir trembled. Tears sprang from his eyes, streamed down his cheeks.

"Don't be afraid," Hub said calmly, almost tenderly. "I can protect you. There's nothing to be afraid of."

"I'm afraid of going to hell," Samir muttered.

He looked as if he thought he'd already arrived there. Hub sat down peacefully, biding his time.

The script he'd worked out with Sharon was paying off. They had Samir right where they wanted him.

Samir forced himself to speak. "His name is Tariq Husseini," he quavered. "He runs an auto shop."

Hub waited for more.

"On Commerce Street in Red Hook," Samir added. Shivering, as if sensing something uncanny—invisible evil—he stared at the air.

Hub scribbled a number on a piece of notepaper. "My beeper number," he informed Samir, handing it over. "Anybody messes with you, I'm there in twenty minutes."

Samir nodded.

Hub patted him on the shoulder. Then he got up and walked out to the hallway.

Sharon was waiting. "You're good," she remarked.

"You're not so . . ."

"Bad yourself," Hub replied, his voice issuing from a speaker in Colonel Hardwick's surveillance van.

The colonel was following the conversation via the CIA's latest microwave audio-probe technology. He heard them walk to the stairs, then down them.

He'd enjoyed listening to Sharon Bridger and

Anthony Hubbard perform their good cop/bad cop routine on Samir Nazhde. He admired it, too; Nazhde had cracked in no time at all. Bridger made an excellent bad cop, Hubbard an adept good cop. The colonel wondered if they were capable of reversing the roles. Somehow he doubted that Hubbard had a sufficiently fierce bad cop in him.

Hardwick looked at the name he'd written on a notepad in his lap: *Tariq Husseini*. The auto shop on Commerce Street in Red Hook soon would get some unexpected new clients.

A minute later Sharon and Hub were sitting in Hub's car. Hub picked up his cell phone and dialed.

"You calling Devereaux?" Sharon asked, dead-pan.

"Didn't get his number," Hub replied, equally deadpan. "Darn."

Sharon smiled faintly. If the general needed Hub, first he was going to have to demonstrate, more convincingly than he had in the command tent, that Hub needed him.

"Floyd," Hub said into the phone. "Hub. We need to put something together in a big-ass hurry." He listened a moment. "Where's Frank? Okay— Good—Give him a 911."

Hub hung up. Sharon checked out the street. A crowd of teenagers watched an armored personnel carrier rumble through. Sharon couldn't explain why, but intuition told her that the scene held trouble. She had her own version of a West Bank sixth sense; something was wrong with the picture before her. A volley of rocks and bottles suddenly hurtled out of nowhere, smashing to no effect against the personnel carriers' flanks. The teenagers laughed and applauded.

But then something exploded up the street. Smoke poured from a car; a small blast had detonated within it. The teenagers' laughs turned to screams. Running wildly, they scattered. Hub jumped out and sprinted to the burning car, pulling his gun from his hip holster. A soldier lay on the pavement, screaming with pain. His leg had been shredded. Blood spurted from the green fatigues, white bone protruded. Hub knelt to examine the wound.

Squealing tires alerted him to the arrival of Jeeps. The soldiers in them locked and loaded M–16s. Before Hub could say a word the rifles were leveled at him. Worse, the soldiers seemed very young. That translated into very inexperienced.

"*FBI!*" Hub shouted. "*FBI!*"

Despite their helmets and rugged combat gear, the kids in the Jeep looked completely at a loss. Scared, confused, probably just weeks out of basic training, they obviously were itching to shoot. At Hub's feet the bloodied soldier kept screaming.

"Now," Hub said very slowly. "I'm gonna . . .

reach . . . into my jacket . . . and show you . . . my shield."

"*Drop your weapon!*" an eighteen-year-old shouted.

Hub dropped his gun. He pulled out his credentials; medics hurried to the wounded man. The kid who'd yelled approached warily. After checking Hub's ID, he said, with real regret, "Sorry, sir." Hub figured he was wondering why more adults with guns weren't in the streets, helping to keep a lid on the mayhem. "Somebody's booby-trapping cars," the soldier explained. "We're all a little spooked."

Hub could see why, and it scared him, too. He was about to say something steadying when small-arms fire rattled farther on down the street. Hub whirled and saw bullets picking up dust, pocking buildings. A window dissolved. In the distance he glimpsed a running figure, three soldiers in pursuit.

All day long Hub had marveled at the mysterious fact that despite his shot nerves, he felt invulnerable. He'd developed a new attitude: Throw whatever you got, because I can take it. His suicide rush down the elementary-school corridor had triggered the turning point. He felt inured now, armored, like the behemoth vehicles rumbling through Brooklyn.

Or so he had thought. He glanced around, at the medics performing emergency surgery on the boy on the pavement, at scared soldiers who'd never before seen this kind of blood, at Sharon staring from the car down the street.

He picked up his gun and walked toward her. *This is it,* Hub thought bleakly. *Brooklyn is Gaza.* Sharon said nothing as he climbed in the car. She was looking at a word on a bullet-scarred wall a few feet from her window.

Graffiti had been newly spray-painted there. Hub stared at it:

INTIFADA.

23

Two hours later Hub and Floyd Rose were driving through Brooklyn in a beat-up old Dodge. Hub wore stained jeans and a baseball cap turned backward. Floyd sported a greasy leather jacket. Few people would have suspected they were conducting the most important business to date of their FBI careers.

Hub passed into Red Hook and turned right on Commerce Street. It served an industrial district that had seen better days; shabby warehouses alternated with shuttered storefronts and overgrown lots. Here the military presence in downtown Brooklyn seemed worlds away. Hub thought about the tanks, APCs, helicopters, and God knew what else flooding into the borough. Even if Red Hook seemed an unlikely target of martial law, other neighborhoods lay prostrate under Bill Devereaux's boot. And by the minute, the situation continued to worsen. The general hadn't been kidding when he announced his intentions for Brooklyn. The squeeze was on.

Hub aimed to change that reality. An elementary task, he told himself wryly. He just had to find the remaining terrorist cells. A piece of cake.

In fact, Hub didn't feel at all confident that Samir's tip would yield the results he wanted. He was angry with himself for not having gotten the information earlier. And he was angry with Elise for having been criminally overprotective of her asset. She could have turned Samir days before, the night they'd picked him up at the smoke-filled café. Hub could have driven to Red Hook then, not now. Without the army's assembled might breathing down his neck.

He parked near the warehouse that housed Tariq Husseini's auto shop. Two winos sharing a bottle lounged on the sidewalk, holding up the warehouse's concrete wall. Hub studied them. Then he activated his walkie-talkie, and said into it, "All units, report in turn. If talking will reveal your position, just key your walkie."

The winos scratched themselves in places they hadn't touched before. As Hub listened to a series of replies, Floyd scanned the warehouse's interior. Young men were operating hoists and compression cylinders. An arc welder emitted blue sparks, sealing a seam in a stripped car. Though the garage couldn't be called orderly—dirty waste barrels and piles of rags gave it a dumplike feel—it plainly was in business. The place looked legitimate.

Hub got out of the Dodge and approached the garage. "Yo," he called to a man working under a car.

The mechanic slid out, his Hispanic face uncurious. "*Que pasa?*" he asked.

Hub said, "Tariq around?"

The man pointed to a partitioned-off office in the rear. Hub headed for it, checking out more workers. Teenagers, from the looks of them. One was doing a compression check. Another was replacing a tire. Hub didn't seem to attract their attention. That, he knew, easily could be a mistaken impression.

Someone was speaking Arabic in the office. Hub entered; a dark-haired man looked up from a table. He was on the phone.

"Tariq?" Hub said.

The man held up a finger, asking Hub to hold on. Hub took a seat opposite.

The phone conversation ended. The man clicked off, and said, "How can I help you?"

"You're Tariq Husseini?" Hub asked.

"He's out," the man said, his eyes hooded.

"Damn," Hub said, not believing the reply. "Do you think you could give him a message?"

"Of course," replied the man, watching Hub closely.

"Tell him the FBI is after him," Hub said with a hard stare.

"You're joking," Tariq Husseini said. Color drained from his face.

"Very slowly," Hub said quietly, "put your hands on the table." Tariq noticed that Hub had placed his own hands under the table. A metallic click sounded there, the unmistakable slide of a semi-automatic.

Tariq muttered an Arabic curse.

Hub inquired, "That wouldn't be a racist epithet, now would it?" Tariq glared. "Stand up," Hub ordered.

Tariq complied. Hub moved behind him and kicked out his legs; Tariq thudded to the floor. Hub patted him down, then cuffed him.

Shouts echoed from the garage. Hub hauled Tariq to his feet and prodded him from the office. The sidewalk winos had produced shotguns. With Floyd Rose, they were rousting the garage workers.

"Where are the others?" Hub asked Tariq.

"What others?" Tariq replied with a sneer.

Hub didn't get a chance to respond. As if issuing from the heavens, an amplified voice boomed: "TARIQ HUSSEINI, THIS IS THE UNITED STATES ARMY. YOU ARE SURROUNDED."

The announcement crashed through the warehouse like an order from God. Tariq gaped, almost seeing the thunderbolt. Hub was equally surprised.

The voice continued: "YOU HAVE THIRTY SECONDS TO THROW OUT ANY WEAPONS AND EXIT THE PREMISES WITH YOUR HANDS ON TOP OF YOUR HEADS."

Near the garage's front, a wino impersonator turned to look at Hub. "Sir?" he said, seeking guidance.

"Do as he says," Hub replied, hustling Tariq forward. Then he saw something that stopped him cold.

One of the teenage mechanics hadn't been handcuffed. His eyes held a murderous glow; with the coiled tension of one who intends to pull a weapon and use it, he reached for an object in his overalls.

The agent tending him noticed this. "Freeze!" he yelled, training his shotgun.

The mechanic froze. Then he extracted his hand. It didn't hold a weapon after all. It held something much worse: a grenade's detonation pin.

The grenade remained in the boy's overalls. But not for long. To Hub, time slowed down.

The explosion shattered the mechanic, flinging limbs and a cloud of guts to the garage's far corners. Both shotgun agents stood within lethal range; first they lost their guns, then their hands, then their faces and hair. Hub watched them disassemble; fragments spewed into the street outside. The prisoners crumpled like tissues in water, hit almost as hard. The garage filled with the metallic scent of blood.

Hub didn't have time to mourn his dead. The military man giving orders would see the explosion as heresy, and grounds for attack. Hub threw Tariq to the floor. Then he dived for cover.

Overhead, gunfire sounded. Someone with a heavy-gauge automatic weapon was raking the street from an upper window. *Damn*, Hub thought. *The army won't take that lying down. They'll return fire with triple the force, at least.*

The bones behind Hub's ears started tingling. Then the white noise stabbed in.

High in a helicopter, General Devereaux inspected the scene via remote-imaging systems. The garage's interior glowed ghostily on screen; smudges indicated where corpses lay, more coherent shapes denoted Hub and his prisoner.

Devereaux keyed controls. On-screen, a targeting grid materialized over the garage image. The general adjusted the grid, designating some areas for attack, excluding others. In moments he had told his forces precisely which places to hit. His eyes narrowed. "Code blue," he said into his microphone.

Hub and Tariq were crawling toward the garage's rear when the projectiles thundered in. Windows exploded, walls peeled, incendiary tracer fire smacked into barrels holding flammable slop. Great gouts of fire leapt to the ceiling; a car's gas tank exploded. The air thickened with searing grit. Tools, tires, and fragmenting objects performed an epileptic ballet.

Hub saw the spectacle, he smelled and felt it, but he couldn't hear anything except white noise. Even as it tormented him, the sound focused his mind. It imbued the scene with a weirdly aesthetic quality: The violence seemed a kind of multimedia show, choreographed to transmute destruction into almost dreamy pirouettes. He glimpsed an M–60 tank gliding noiselessly into position out front. Its turret swiveled, bringing muzzles to bear. Something flashed to it from the warehouse's upper floor, leaving a fiery trail. A rocket-propelled grenade: It hit, and the tank bloomed surreally, a futurist orchid unfurling flames.

Devereaux watched it all from the chopper, coldly fascinated. He felt himself to be an artist at times like this. He was creating a masterpiece: composing, conducting, and playing instruments all at once. It gave meaning to life. More than that, actually. It *was* life.

"Code red," he told his microphone.

Hub crawled across the garage floor, dragging Tariq, whose deadweight indicated either unconsciousness or paralytic fright. Ahead, doors offered a way out. Above the doors a jagged hole framed blue sky and the upper stories of tenement buildings. Hub happened to glance through the hole just when the military made its next move.

Like movie monsters silently breaking the surface of a pond, then rearing to strike at an unsuspecting victim, two machines rose from a hiding place behind the tenement buildings. Apache attack helicopters, Hub perceived. They swooped toward the warehouse, their high-caliber machine guns glowing orange. Spitting two thousand rounds a minute, Hub recalled from his time in the 82nd Airborne.

The bullets unzipped the building. What had survived the earlier fusillades, now gave way; the garage and everything in it began to decompose to material the consistency of slag.

That proved to be just a softening-up for the grand finale. High-yield Hydra rockets ignited in the Apaches' weapons pods. Hub watched them home in, not hearing their exhausts' deadly *whoosh*. *This is it,* he thought. *Now or never.*

He heaved Tariq to his feet and pulled him through the doors. Tariq did hear the rockets. The sound evoked uncherished memories of his youth in southern Lebanon; suddenly he regained his ability to move. The two men staggered out.

Behind them the entire warehouse erupted into

a massive fireball, orange tessellated with oily black smoke.

Devereaux, calmly detached, watched the fireball climb. His symphony had come to a satisfactory conclusion. Particularly because Hub and Tariq Husseini had emerged just in time.

It seemed like swimming through liquid mercury, trying to outrun the fireball. Without the white noise it would have been a daunting experience. With the white noise in full crescendo, Hub felt as if hell itself were licking at his heels.

He was almost grateful when the commandos seized him.

24

At the meeting in the Broadway theater where law-enforcement officials had gathered following the destruction of the Federal Building, Danny Sussman asked a logistical question to which no one had supplied an answer: Where on earth would the authorities place something like sixteen hundred detainees?

Night had fallen over New York City. Hub, in fresh clothes and cleansed of fireball residue, stared at the answer to Danny's question. The favorite mass-detention choice of repressive regimes and newly minted juntas all over the world loomed before him: a football stadium.

Armored personnel carriers and tanks ringed the enormous structure. An antiterrorist perimeter bolstered security: fences of razor-tipped concertina wire to thwart escape attempts, concrete obstacles and walls of sandbags to discourage vehicular attacks. Musco lights shone from newly erected towers, filling the parking areas and roadways around the stadium with a pitiless glow.

Hub approached the one checkpoint providing access through the perimeter to the stadium. A mob of furious parents, girlfriends, advocates, and community leaders milled about, trying to contend with a situation that hadn't existed in America since the Second World War, when Japanese-American citizens were confined in the camps at Manzanar.

Manzanar had long since been considered a profoundly un-American aberration, a disgrace that required formal governmental apologies and reparations. Nonetheless, here it had resurrected in New York, this time with a different ethnicity as the target.

Hub pressed through the mob to the checkpoint. A man was berating the young lieutenant in charge: "I just want to find out if my client *is on the list.*"

An ACLU lawyer, Hub guessed. The man had the look: idealistic and outraged. Hub would want the fellow on his side.

The lieutenant said, "Sir, the list will be updated every twelve hours and posted in the . . ."

A pack of journalists, brandishing microphones and notepads, forced their way through. "This pass *guarantees access!*" one bellowed. "The *First fucking*

Amendment," another snarled. "You can't *do* this!" an imperious woman proclaimed.

The lieutenant fought to keep his temper. "There will be a pool briefing for all accredited journalists at 0700 hours," he announced.

Hub showed his ID. The lieutenant waved him through.

A dark tunnel led directly to the stadium's arena. Hub walked down it, his footsteps echoing, his gorge threatening to rise. In the course of doing his job over the years he had encountered numerous situations that could best be summed up, at the most basic level, as disgusting. Rarely had any evoked more disgust than what he felt now.

A whimper echoed through the darkness. Hub squinted, trying to find the source. He couldn't make out anything, and moved along.

He emerged into a tableau that would stay with him for the rest of his life. The estimate of sixteen hundred detainees looked to be short of the mark. At least two thousand men were spread out on the halogen-lit football field, all between the ages of sixteen and thirty. They squatted, they smoked, they paced; some seemed lighthearted, cracking jokes and laughing. Most simply looked terrified.

Hub glanced up at the stands. The higher tiers bristled with the silhouettes of armed guards. Machine-gun emplacements were brightly lit, unshy about making themselves known. Exits had been barricaded. Surveillance towers swept the arena with electronic eyes and ears.

On the ground, enlisted men operated food and shelter stations, passing out soup, blankets, and other basic necessities. Hub glimpsed a familiar figure standing not far away: Tina Osu, her face stilled with disbelief.

Hub went to her. Tina acknowledged him with a flicker of an eyelash. She tried to say something, but couldn't. Hub cleared his throat. He himself was at a loss for words.

Tina murmured, "In 1942, my father was put into the camps at Manzanar. Until the end of the war. Two years. Now he roots for the Dodgers and swears it could never happen again."

Hub nodded. It was happening again. And unless he salvaged something from the unholy funeral pyre that Devereaux had made of Tariq Husseini's auto shop, he didn't think he could do a damn thing about it. He wanted to comfort Tina. He wanted to catch his breath and begin to grapple with the decimation of the agents under his command. Reach out to their families, for God's sake. Arrange for the appropriate Bureau contributions to the services.

For now, though, all that had to wait. He exchanged a few words with Tina and headed across the field.

A corporal informed him that he could find

Devereaux somewhere behind something that looked like a thick mesh fence. On closer inspection it turned out to be hundreds of wire cages. An aisle led through them. *Brigs for the unruly,* Hub thought with detachment. *No doubt soon to be filled.*

Someone burst from the shadows, looking crazed. Hub felt a sudden jolt as he recognized Frank Haddad. He'd never seen Frank in such a state. The man literally looked murderous.

"They got Frankie," Frank blurted. "My *kid's* here someplace . . ."

Hub put a hand on Frank's shoulder. "Frank, slow down," he said.

Frank blinked away tears of rage. "He's only *thirteen*, for Chrissake!"

Off in the distance a liturgical voice chanted, "*Allahuh Akbar!*" Even here, Hub thought, or especially here, holy men called the faithful to prayer. "I'll get him out," he told Frank with feeling.

"They came into my *house*," Frank exclaimed. "Najiba told them who I was—" He swallowed hard. "How many times did I put it on the line, Hub? *How many times?*"

"Frank," Hub said urgently, a note of pleading in his voice. It destroyed him to see his right-hand man this way.

"We're American citizens, twenty years," Frank ranted. "Ten years in the Bureau—they *knocked her down*. And took him. Out of my own house."

"It's wrong, Frank," Hub declared. "What can I say to you, but it's all—*terribly, horribly*—wrong." He took Frank's arm. "Now, come with me."

Frank pulled away. "*No!*" he shouted. "I've got to find him. Besides, this is where I belong." He pulled out his wallet, extracted his badge, and surrendered it to Hub. "Here. I'm not their sand nigger anymore."

Hub watched Frank walk away to the crowd of prisoners. Again the *muezzin* chanted the call to prayers. Frank dropped to his knees, joining the worship.

Devereaux still waited beyond the wire cages. Hub turned to find him.

The general had set up his command post in a locker room. Computers, phones, and security monitors looked out of place in a setting that smelled of deodorant, bleach, and laundry. So did the bustling hierarchy of military staff.

Hub was admitted to an inner area. Colonel Hardwick and Devereaux looked up as he entered. Hub dispensed with pleasantries that would have been far from pleasant even to think, never mind utter. "You've taken into custody the son of one of my men," he told the general. "The name is Frank Haddad, Junior. I want him now."

Devereaux smiled. "His name is Haddad?" he asked.

"*Frank* Haddad," Hub snapped. "Junior."

"His father's a Shiite," Hardwick remarked. "We're checking him out."

Hub shoved Frank's badge under Hardwick's nose. "Check *this* out, pal. His father's a federal agent for ten years."

"Don't get in my face, Hubbard," Hardwick said icily. "I might decide you're an Ethiopian."

Hub's eyes widened. "And you're just stupid enough to think that's an insult," he said, amazed.

"If a mistake's been made," Devereaux interjected, "we'll fix it."

"There is no 'if,'" Hub insisted. "I'm vouching for this kid. I want him out!"

"And I said we'll look into it," Devereaux replied.

"You mean," Hub expostulated, "like you're looking into *me*? Surveilling me? Breaking up my operations? If I'd known I was going to be doing your job for you, I would never have left the army!"

Devereaux said tonelessly, "There's an FBI office in Anchorage, Agent Hubbard. Fuck with me, and you'll be learning a hundred and fifty new words for snow."

They glared at each other. "Tariq Husseini is my prisoner," Hub informed the general. "I want to see him."

"The prisoner is being interrogated," Devereaux replied with bland self-assurance.

I bet, Hub thought, even more determined to check out Tariq. What were these guys doing to him? "I want to see him," he repeated.

Tariq was being held in a shower room. An appropriate place, with built-in features to clean away mess, Hub reflected as he studied the man's condition. Tariq sat naked on a folding metal chair, secured with straps. His head lolled on his chest, his eyes dull, a strand of saliva dangling from the corner of his mouth. A nearby table held a hypodermic syringe, its plunger depressed, recently used. Two MPs stood guard.

But the most arresting feature of the interrogation was the identity of the interrogator. Sharon Bridger sat across from Tariq. She was speaking to him, softly, in Arabic.

Tariq appeared not to hear her. Then, suddenly, his head jerked up. He spat, hitting Sharon squarely in the face.

She wiped away the spittle as if it were a droplet of rainwater. Sharon was accustomed to this, Hub observed. She'd done it before.

General Devereaux asked her, "How long have you been at it?"

"Not long enough, apparently," Sharon replied. She looked at Tariq with clinical objectivity.

"How much longer, do you think, before he gives up the other cells?" Devereaux pressed.

Hub pointed out, "He can't give up the other cells if he doesn't know about them."

"He knows," Devereaux said with certainty.

Hub gestured at Sharon, and said, "What about her briefing? The strategy session at the Capitol—she said the cells don't know about each other, that they—"

Devereaux ignored Hub. "How long before he breaks?" he asked Sharon pointedly.

"At this rate," Sharon said. She looked up. "Too long. The theater was hit nine hours after we took down the first cell."

"So . . ." Devereaux said with a reflective frown. "What other models do we have?"

Sharon considered the question, as if reviewing a mental checklist of "models." Hub wondered how far they went. How proficient Sharon was at executing them? What measures she was prepared to take to make someone talk?

"Shaking," Devereaux suggested. No one had a response to the idea. The general sighed impatiently. "What about it, Sharon?"

"Won't work," Sharon said.

"Works for the Israelis," Devereaux remarked, his eyes hardening.

"Only in conjunction with sleep deprivation," Sharon replied with matter-of-fact calm. "Needs at least thirty-six hours."

Hub stared at Sharon, seeing confirmation of

his worst suspicions. The woman wasn't merely conversant with theories of how to elicit information with force. She practiced them; she had derived her knowledge from personal experience.

"We don't have thirty-six hours," Devereaux said, exasperation evident in his voice.

Silence fell. Hub realized that a line was about to be crossed. Beyond the line lay a moral chasm.

"Electric shock?" Devereaux proposed.

"The neurotransmitters just shut down," Sharon said dismissively.

"Water?" Devereaux said in a louder tone of voice.

Colonel Hardwick spoke up. "Palestinian Authority is producing good intel using water," he said with a note of admiration.

Hub could take it no longer. "Are you people insane?" he demanded.

Devereaux cocked an eye at Hub. "The time has come," he said slowly, "for one man to suffer in order to save the lives of thousands."

"How about *two* men?" Hub asked. "How about *three*? How about public executions, that might work!"

"You're welcome to wait outside," Devereaux said with ominous indifference.

"General," Hub said, waving an arm. "You've lost men, I've lost men. But we gotta . . ." A disturbing insight flashed through his mind. "What if . . ." Hub groped for the implications. "What if they don't want their leader back at all? You said yourself, we don't even have him. Maybe what they *really* want . . ." Hub grasped the insight more clearly; it seemed to spread evil wings. "I think they *want* us to herd our children into stadiums," he declared. "Put soldiers into our streets. Radicalize people who want to think of themselves as Americans. Bend the law, shred the Constitution. Because if we torture him," Hub went on, "and let's call it what it is"—he nodded at the slumped Tariq Husseini—"you, and I"—Hub shook his head—"then the country that men like us have sworn to defend, and bled to defend, and died to defend—is gone." He paused, took a deep breath. "And they've won."

Devereaux wasn't prepared to take seriously the possibility that the terrorists might have a plan into which he was playing; he couldn't conceive of himself, and the army, getting caught in a trap. The idea just didn't fly in his hardwired brain. Nor could the general tolerate a scenario the end game of which involved the words, "They've won." Such words might apply to the failed strategies of lesser commanders fighting lesser battles. But they never would apply to the enemy in any war *he* was fighting. The general turned to Colonel Hardwick. Conversationally, he said, "I think we have to soundproof the room before we begin."

Hub said, "He's my prisoner. I'm taking him out of your jurisdiction."

For the first time in the memory of anyone present, Devereaux lost control. "*Get him out of here!*" he roared with a sweep of his arm, the force of which left no doubt as to how the ejection should be executed.

The two MPs pounced on Hub. He didn't resist; they hustled him out to a corridor and slammed him down hard on a plain pine bench. Colonel Hardwick followed. For a moment he stood over Hub, regarding him with a mixture of contempt and undisguised loathing. Then he returned to the shower room. The MPs locked the door and took up sentry positions on either side. They weren't going anywhere. Nor was Tariq Husseini. Geographically, that is; Tariq faced a journey the destination of which remained in the experienced hands of Sharon Bridger.

Hub wearily rubbed his eyes. He had to think. But not here. To try to get a grip anywhere near here invited self-pollution.

Hours later, the corridor was empty. The MPs had gone, others had gone as well. Devereaux, mindful of the taboo he was breaking, had decided to minimize witnesses.

The door to the shower room unlocked from within. Sharon emerged looking as if she herself had just suffered an extended bout of torture. And in a sense, she had. Her bloodless face and enfeebled gait suggested that, emotionally, she was shattered. Something burdened her with terrible weight: the sins she had helped perpetrate beyond the door.

A gunshot rang out in there. Tiled walls and floors amplified the report, giving it finality, but not closure. Only the finality of an ugly and haunting death.

Devereaux came out, like Sharon, wrung to the bone.

"He knew nothing," Sharon said.

Devereaux's shoulders sagged. He turned and walked away, lacking his customary verve. Having just come eyeball-to-eyeball with his own honor, he had done the unthinkable. General William Devereaux had blinked.

25

Hub devoted much of the next day to consolidating his forces. Morale had become a problem; everyone, himself included, needed reminders that grief was a luxury when waging war. He also launched a discreet investigation into Colonel Hardwick's Army Intelligence operation. The colonel was tracking him closely. Everything Hub did, whatever he unearthed, was landing on Devereaux's desk. Hub wanted to know how the process worked. Until he found out and took countermeasures, he would serve the general's agenda, which posed a problem. Hub refused to give up on the case; no matter how long the odds, he had do what he could to find the remaining terrorist cells. But he couldn't tolerate functioning as Devereaux's pawn. Tariq Husseini's fate made that morally unacceptable.

The ability to outflank Hardwick thus had become a priority. The FBI didn't possess the sophisticated new microwave surveillance tools that Hardwick no doubt was using. But Hub's people had two assets the colonel's agents lacked: street-smart savvy about Brooklyn's complex urban fabric and the borough's profound resentment of the army's attitudes and methods.

As the day wore on Hub's decision began to pay off. Reports came in on the equipment, vehicles, and personnel under Hardwick's command.

In the early evening he got a phone call from Washington. Someone important wanted to see him as soon as possible. A plane was waiting at La Guardia.

Hub didn't want to make the trip. But considering who had called, he really had no choice.

At Reagan National Airport, Hub declined the use of the official car available to him. A rental suited him better. It lessened the possibility of bugs. What he'd been learning about Hardwick made him quite wary of the government's willingness to use them.

Before heading to Georgetown and his appointment, he drove around a while taking in some sights. Washington at night provided any number of spectacular treats for the eye. The floodlit major monuments interested Hub in particular: the soaring obelisk dedicated to George himself, Thomas Jefferson's domed temple, and, most significant of all to Hub, the colonnaded edifice in which sat the majestically rendered marble statue of Abraham Lincoln.

Hub stared at the Lincoln statue from his rental car. Since childhood he'd revered this sight. It symbolized all that was good and just and free.

All that the terrorists, and William Devereaux, were not.

At eight o'clock sharp he pulled up before a lovely town house in Georgetown. Hub noted an unmarked car parked nearby. The two men in it were Secret Service agents, keeping vigil.

Todd Franklin, the White House chief of staff, opened the door. He wore a Dartmouth varsity lacrosse T-shirt and looked surprisingly like a regular family man, despite his position and evident affluence. In the background, a three-year-old squalled.

"C'mon in," Franklin said affably. "We're still trying to get the last one down."

Franklin led Hub to the living room. Children's toys and rag rugs mingled with tasteful antiques, more evidence of well-to-do domesticity. The sight reminded Hub of his single status. His lack of little ones. Franklin looked to be a grounded guy. A more pretentious man wouldn't receive visitors, even people subordinate by the huge margin that separated Franklin from Hub, in such relaxed circumstances.

They sat. Franklin got right to business. "The

president wants this shit over with," he announced, staring at the floor. "There's only one way to do that." He looked up at Hub, directly in the eye. "Let the sheik go."

Hub wasn't surprised. He remained capable of feeling shock, and did, a little; but somehow he just wasn't surprised. He said, to make sure he was getting this right, "So we *do* have the sheik?"

"You think our government operates as a single coherent entity?" Franklin asked. "Devereaux just . . ." He paused, considering how to put it. "Pushed the agenda."

That didn't surprise Hub at all.

"Of course," Franklin added circumspectly, "the president was completely unaware of it."

"Of course," Hub echoed, hitting the ball back across the net. Presidents made sure they never knew about outrageously illegal acts committed by their senior appointees, even when they did know. In recent years presidential knowledge had become a slippery phenomenon. Subject to hairsplitting debate.

"Now we can't just let him go," Franklin continued. "America has to stand tall in the world, yadda, yadda, yadda. So what we do is . . ."

Hub waited to hear it, wondering what role he would be asked to play, and wondering further if he "needed to know" any of this. Franklin's drift was beginning to sound toxic.

His wife entered the room, holding the crying child. A contest was under way. Mrs. Franklin, a handsome woman showing signs of wear, wasn't winning. "Honey—" she said, clearly needing backup.

"I'll be right up, darling," Franklin said firmly.

Mrs. Franklin gritted her teeth, suppressing complaints. She turned and left.

Hub inferred that the domesticity here wasn't so relaxed after all.

"You have kids?" Franklin asked Hub. "They're great. Sometimes you just want to . . . drug 'em."

Hub stayed on track. He asked, "What do you mean, let the justice system do its work?"

"We don't release the sheik," Franklin replied. "A judge releases him." He waved a hand. "You're an FBI man. That's what judges are good at, right?"

Hub had dealt with obstinate judges, most recently Abraham Frankel, but he objected to dumping the blame for this crisis in the judiciary's lap. It didn't strike him as taking responsibility.

Franklin caught the look in Hub's eyes. "It's not like we've gone after him in proper prosecutorial fashion," he pointed out. "Kidnapping him. Holding him in isolation. 'Fruit of the poisoned tree'— remember that one from law school?" Franklin smiled. "Oh, we'll have a big trial. Everybody'll get their rocks off. But the fact is"—he inhaled deeply—"the sheik will walk."

Hub recalled the terrorists' faxed messages: RELEASE HIM. He had to give one thing to Todd Franklin and the president. They knew when to cry uncle.

Franklin shook his head. "And this whole episode becomes nothing more than the news cycle before the next news cycle," he remarked.

Is that all? Hub thought. Franklin's cynicism astounded him.

The chief of staff picked up a thick accordion file. "Documentary evidence of Devereaux's whole operation," he announced with finality. He handed the file to Hub.

"Why me?" Hub asked.

"Because you'll know what to do with it," Franklin replied.

Hub hefted the file in his hands. It felt potent, capable of doing damage. He wasn't sure he wanted anything to do with it. "And what about her?" he asked, raising a subject that couldn't be avoided. Given what Franklin was asking him to do.

"Who?" Franklin inquired innocently.

"You know who," Hub replied, unafraid to let his impatience show. "How much is she complicit in all this?"

Franklin shrugged. "Ask her," he said.

Hub looked up. Sharon Bridger stood in the front hallway. She had been listening to the entire conversation.

*   *   *

Hub and Sharon drove through Georgetown streets, silently taking in the antique architecture, the walls enclosing private gardens, the neighborhood's understated claim to entitlement and privilege. Many powerful people lived here. Some would crash, others would thrive; divining which would happen to whom constituted one of Washington's most vital pastimes. To the uninitiated, Georgetown could be misleading about that fact. It took time to learn just how much ruthlessness resided behind the pretty brick facades.

Hub had little experience with bringing down the high-and-mighty. He wanted to ask Sharon about the accordion file now stashed in his trunk. Had Franklin received it from her? How deep was she in the decision to blame the sheik's release on the courts? And make Devereaux the fall guy for a misguided policy that others, more senior, had approved?

She didn't bring those topics up. Nor did Hub raise them. At the moment he wasn't inclined to help Sharon explain herself. That she could grapple with on her own. As far as he was concerned, he would remain silent however long it took for her to crack.

And eventually she would crack, Hub knew. Sharon's unflappability had eroded. The stonewall looked shaky tonight; Hub could see it in her fidgety hands, hear it in occasional sighs that surfaced.

When she started talking her tone was brisk. "I ran an Iraqi network for two years," she remarked, as if volunteering a straightforward résumé. "Samir recruited them from among the sheik's followers. I trained them in the north. Then we played them back into Baghdad, two, three at time, hiding them in the mosques."

Hub nodded. This much he'd already gathered.

"It was gonna be beautiful," Sharon said in a softer tone. She stared wistfully through her window. "And then," she added, her voice developing a catch, "there was a policy shift." She shivered at the memory. Hub realized she was having trouble exhuming this long-dead subject; probably she hadn't known how volatile her feelings about it were. *That's what you get,* he thought darkly. *When the job requires buried emotions.*

Sharon sighed. "The new doctrine was: Iran will be too powerful if Iraq falls apart." She wrung her hands; her voice trembled as she added, "And it's not like we sold them out. Exactly. We just stopped . . ." She glared through the windshield. "Helping them. And I wasn't allowed to tell them what was coming down. I was ordered *not* to tell them." Suddenly she was fighting back tears. "And they got slaughtered."

Hell of a position to be in, Hub reflected.

"You've got to understand," she went on, her

eyes brighter as more memories fed the fire. "These people *believe*. Paradise. Bliss. To us they're just words, but to them . . ." Again she sighed. "It's very beautiful, actually. And when you look at their lives, the heartbreak . . ." She shuddered, appalled at the interior landscape of her past. "And what do we do? We think, *Aha*. We can take advantage of *that*." She started crying.

Hub pulled over. Sharon in tears he classified as a driving hazard.

"So I *quit*," Sharon moaned, rivulets flowing down her face. "I came home. I just can't . . . do it . . . anymore."

She grimaced, annoyed with herself for making this display, angry that she was exposing Hub to her vulnerabilities. Hub felt moved in spite of himself. He put his arms around her, patted her back. She shuddered within his embrace. As if revolted at the idea of clinging.

It occurred to Hub that he was holding a beautiful, dangerous predator. "But first, you helped them," he said, surprising himself with the directness of his tone.

She withdrew from his arms, looked up through her tears. Gamely, she tried to regain the imperturbable face. "What do you mean?" she whispered.

"They were being slaughtered," Hub reminded her. "They needed to get out. But," he went on, raising something that had bothered him ever since the State Department had told him to call INS, and INS had ping-ponged him back to State, "they were on the Watch List." The list that supposedly screened out terrorists. "So you got them visas. You and Samir."

Sharon heard the accusation in Hub's voice. She didn't want to acknowledge it. "I promised we would take care of them," shaking her head, as if affronted. "They were working *for us*."

"Doing what, exactly?" Hub demanded. He pulled back out into traffic.

"I don't know what you mean," Sharon said, trying to maintain the fiction that her actions had been exemplary.

"You said you trained them," Hub said, reminding her further. "Tradecraft. Subversion. That's what you said, right?" He gave her a sharp sidelong glance. Sharon nodded, her nostrils flaring. "Only you left something out, didn't you?" Hub went on. "*Didn't you*, Sharon?"

She couldn't look at him now. She bit her lower lip.

Hub delivered the coup de grâce. "You taught them how to make bombs."

Sharon started crying again, harder than before. Her head jerked with an affirmative nod.

"And now they're here, doing what you taught 'em," Hub observed, pointing out what was finally obvious.

A streetlight washed over Sharon's face, catching the haunted look in her eyes. She murmured, "And I'm going to have to live with the hell of that for the rest of my life."

Hub almost felt sorry for her. He now knew with greater certainty than ever that Sharon had made a fatal mistake. She had allowed empathy for her assets to get in the way. Hub recalled what Sharon had mentioned at the bar where they'd blown off steam the night after the pizza-delivery takedown: "My father used to say they seduce you with their suffering."

Suffering had seduced Sharon Bridger. In her own fashion she was almost as complicit with the terrorism crisis as the sheik. And certainly as complicit as Bill Devereaux.

Hub didn't envy the position Sharon would occupy if those facts became public. He thought a bit more and realized that "if" probably was a bit too optimistic. The bombs that Sharon had helped bring into being eventually would catch up with her. The woman hadn't just put others in jeopardy. She, too, very likely was doomed.

She seemed to know that. She even seemed to accept her responsibility. The root of her need to be hurt?

26

The next day brought heightened jitters to Brooklyn and the rest of New York City. Over thirty-six hours had passed since the terrorists' last killings, the losses that the army and FBI had suffered during the assault on the auto shop. Furthermore, the terrorists hadn't planned those deaths. It was beginning to look as if they had suspended their cycle of escalation and retribution. Why? Had the auto-shop inferno knocked them out? Or were they biding their time, waiting for an opportune moment to make their next, even more damaging move?

Only they knew. But their inactivity had its own effect. The authorities couldn't point at fresh blood to justify the Brooklyn lockup that continued to tighten. And people were getting increasingly fed up.

Talk radio roiled with condemnation. New

Yorkers breakfasted that morning to the sounds of angry voices calling for action:

"The people of Brooklyn will not be held hostage! This afternoon, join community and religious leaders in a march to protest the mass arrests!"

Hub and Sharon drove through an Arab neighborhood near Brooklyn's downtown, taking in the mood of near rebellion. Small children loitered, shouting obscenities at patrolling troops. Banners bewailing missing sons and fathers hung from windows. Militant women passed out newsletters, street vendors hawked special editions of the city's Arabic tabloids. The situation's core fact stood out everywhere, evident not as a presence but an absence: The streets were virtually devoid of adolescent boys and young men.

Hub parked near an apartment building where Sharon had scheduled a meeting with Samir. The army wasn't detaining him, which meant that Hardwick had him under surveillance with a thoroughness bordering on the proctological. Hub, of course, had taken that into account.

He and Sharon got out of the car. Teenage girls clustered on the sidewalk, their faces defiantly veiled in the traditional Arab manner—yet another sign of the populace's radicalization, its drift toward Islam's more reactionary precepts. Just days before, only a small minority of the area's women had worn *keffiyehs* and other head coverings. Fashion-conscious kids were sporting them now. Old customs had come back in vogue as a political statement.

That didn't augur well for the city, Hub feared. Fundamentalism would only breed more terror, more zealots willing to die as martyrs. The girls jeered a passing Jeep, shouting taunts and obscene curses. Hub tried to imagine another week of this. Molotov cocktails flaming in the streets?

On the corner an earnest middle-aged man was handing out leaflets. "Two o'clock!" he cried. "March on City Hall! *No fear!*"

Something exploded up the street. Everyone froze a fraction of a second. Then the girls screamed and scattered. The sidewalk emptied.

Hub drew his gun. Smoke billowed from a car in the next block; he dashed to it. A soldier lay on the pavement writhing in agony. He'd received what had come to be routine wounds: a shattered lower body. *It's like land mines,* Hub thought with revulsion. Booby-trapped cars had become the urban equivalent of mines, striking without warning.

Jeeps converged, soldiers pointing rifles from them. "FBI!" Hub yelled at nervous young faces under the helmets. A sensation of *déjà vu* washed through him; day before yesterday he had confronted M–16s in exactly the same circumstances.

The wounded soldier howled; blood eddied to the curb. Hub said slowly to the men in the Jeeps, "I'm gonna reach into my jacket. And show you. My shield."

"Drop your weapon!" a soldier barked.

Hub complied. As he pulled his ID, the soldier approached. Medics rushed to the wounded man. "Somebody's booby-trapping cars," the soldier muttered after a glance at Hub's badge. "Spooking us to hell . . ."

Hub nodded. In the distance, soldiers chased a running boy. *It won't be a week before Molotovs started flaming. The cocktails are already here.*

Early in the afternoon Frank met Hub and Sharon on the fringes of Cadman Plaza near Borough Hall. Hub had secured Frank Jr.'s release from the stadium the day before, with the result that Frank Sr., to Hub's great relief, was back on the job.

A march organizer handed out leaflets down the way. "March on City Hall," he chanted in a refrain that was being repeated all over the city. "No fear!"

Borough Hall dominated the plaza. A stark Greek Revival mass with an imposing stairway and a Victorian cupola, it had been City Hall prior to New York's absorption of Brooklyn, and in the minds of some residents, many decades later, still deserved its old name. The plaza itself was developed in the 1950s. It retained the look of that period. Across it stood the massive Federal Courthouse where Judge Abraham Frankel conducted business.

The protest march would begin in just over an hour, with a rally on Borough Hall's steps. The organizers were expecting a huge turnout. So did the media. TV news trucks already dotted the plaza.

Hub had chosen this location to rendezvous not despite the open layout, but because of it. Hardwick's technicians would have trouble finding positions from which to train their parabolic probes; the surveillance vans couldn't get close enough without giving themselves away. At this point, Hub's people had identified the vans, and Hub knew where they were. But Hardwick didn't know that Hub knew that; Hardwick's ignorance would limit his options.

Hub wanted to minimize what the colonel could see and hear with regard to activities going on in his car. He stood on one side of it, Frank on the other. Together they blocked lines of sight to the interior.

Sharon sat there, performing minor surgery on Samir. The radio played loudly, another measure to foil remote eavesdropping. Samir winced as Sharon's scalpel cut a small incision under his arm. "Ahhhhh," he moaned.

"In case you decide to go on walkabout," Sharon told him. She took a tiny plastic transmitter from a sterile pouch. With confidence that bespoke experience, she inserted the transmitter into the incision. "How did you make contact?" she asked her patient.

What she and Hub had been hoping for seemed to have come to pass. Samir claimed to have been told that only one terrorist cell remained. The men in it were prepared to meet with him.

"He is Afghani," Samir replied. "*Ahhhhh* . . . He got word to my uncle at the bathhouse. You never met him."

"But you're sure he'll show up," Sharon said. She threaded a surgical needle to suture the incision.

Samir trembled. "Sharon," he said as she applied the first stitch, "they are all dead but the last cell, and they are *crazy with fear*. Just tell me the message, and I will pass it on."

"I need to deliver it in person," Sharon said. "Believe me, they'll want to hear what I have to say." She completed the stitching. Then she turned off the radio, signaling to Hub that Samir was all set.

Hub and Frank continued to flank the car. "You watch the game?" Hub asked casually, showing Frank a slip of paper. On it he'd scribbled: *Hit Hardwick. Safe house.*

Frank registered the note and nodded. "Too bad Seahorn is out for the season," he remarked.

Hub wrote a second note. *"Bathhouse, later."*

Frank nodded again. "Think they'll make the playoffs?" he asked.

Hub shot Frank a look that held more than business; for way too long he'd had no time to chat about sports or anything else relating to fun. "How's your boy?" he asked.

Frank cracked a faint smile. "He's all right," he replied. "Thanks for getting him out."

Sharon emerged from the car holding a small device. It featured a display on which a blinking green dot appeared. Sharon indicated the dot. "That's Samir," she said.

Hub studied the portable oscilloscope, then peered into the car at Samir. "Green is about right," he said, referring to Samir's state of mind. He slipped the notes to Sharon.

"He's terrified," she said as she read the scribbles. "Then again, so am I."

"You sure he'll go through with it?" Hub asked. Samir's track record didn't highlight sincerity.

"If he doesn't," Sharon replied, "he knows I'll give him to Devereaux." Soundlessly she mouthed, *They out there?* Hub nodded. "How's it feel to be on the other end of it?" Sharon asked.

She was reminding Hub that she herself had been on the other end, the nights that Hub had trained binoculars on her apartment window. "I like watching better," he told her.

Sharon said sharply, "This is the end game, you understand that? If this goes wrong . . ."

Hub declared, "Nothing's going wrong." He wished he really felt so sure.

"We're the CIA; something *always* goes wrong," Sharon retorted. The car door opened. Samir stepped out, buttoning his shirt. "I don't suppose," Sharon said, "there's any way you would trust me to do this on my own?"

The look on Hub's face said, Never in a million years.

"I thought not," Sharon said with a philosophical shrug. "Well, in case it gets hairy, remember— the most committed wins."

Hub wondered if that meant they had a problem. Sharon's commitment, he now knew, flowed from turbid regions of her soul. He watched her and Samir walk away.

Frank said, "I trust her about as far as I can throw her."

"That far?" Hub said. He wasn't being flip; he sounded truly amazed.

Sharon and Samir hurried through the plaza. "This is not the way to the bathhouse," Samir said with agitation, his eyes darting right and left. "You said to get a key from my uncle so that we . . ."

"*Shhhhh. . . .*" Sharon hissed. They reached an intersection. The pedestrian crossing sign said WALK, but she grabbed Samir's elbow to stop him. "If you'd stop whining, you'd feel the . . ."

". . . surveillance," Sharon admonished.

Colonel Hardwick, wearing earphones, listened to Sharon and Samir in his van.

Samir didn't reply. Sharon said, "Wait for the light to turn yellow, then cross against the traffic."

Hardwick's computer screen displayed a grid map of Brooklyn. He said into his microphone, "North on Ditmas Avenue."

A corporal sitting beside the colonel studied a status screen. "Sound garden's ready," he reported.

The "sound garden" the corporal mentioned consisted of a triangulated field of mobile microphones deployed in the area around Sharon and Samir. From a nearby rooftop, an army spotter trained a parabolic device fitted with a gunsight. Another microphone absorbed sound from a woman's shopping bag. The third rode in a twenty-year-old's boom box. Each mike fed a continuous stream of acoustical data to computers in Hardwick's van. Military software sorted the data, extracting from it astonishingly clear audio of Sharon and Samir's conversation.

"Sharon, I cannot do this thing," Samir was saying. "They are all dead but the last cell, and they are crazy with fear. What is the difference if you burn me or they kill me? Either way I am a dead man."

"Tell them you're bringing a hostage," Sharon suggested.

Samir said despairingly, "I'm sure they would love to meet you, Sharon. But only so they could kill you."

"So be it," she said. "Now wait for the light."

"They are watching?" Samir asked.

The light turned red. Sharon prompted Samir. They raced across the street in a blare of horns from laterally approaching traffic, cars that had just gotten a green signal.

No cops were around to ticket the jaywalkers. Sharon led Samir to a building. They ducked into a side entrance, then ran down a long emergency stairwell. Samir held his tongue; he had no idea where they were going, but Sharon seemed to. They passed through a parking garage, took an elevator to a shopping concourse, then emerged near an apartment building. Sharon used a key to gain entry to another side door. From there it was a short journey to a CIA "clean" apartment, one that agents had swept for bugs.

Samir recognized the place, for he had visited it before. In the living room Sharon turned on the TV and cranked up the volume. "How soon will they come?" she asked Samir. She referred to the *ham-*

mam, an Arab bathhouse, where the meeting was to convene.

"Soon enough," he replied.

The TV was carrying local news, news that in fact was garnering a worldwide audience. Protest marchers had gathered in front of Borough Hall. A speaker on the steps exhorted the crowd: "We will not be made afraid to walk free in this great city. I say, march across the bridge and into the stadium. Demand the release of . . ."

Samir gazed at the image. "So tragic," he murmured in a tone that drew Sharon's attention.

She stared at the protesters. "Not the march," she said apprehensively.

Samir nodded. "Arab and Jew, side by side. Black and white, Christian and Muslim . . ."

"So American," Samir continued, his voice issuing from Colonel Hardwick's microwave screen, his body a spectral glow. Sharon's body glowed beside him. "Could they ever dare to imagine a better target?" he asked, his tone both regretful and mocking.

Hardwick grabbed a secure cell phone. "Get me Devereaux," he barked.

27

Hub walked through Cadman Plaza, on an errand he'd been thinking about since his visit to the football stadium gulag. The crowd had grown considerably in front of Borough Hall. A fiery speaker was whipping it up, inciting the protesters with rhetorical questions about the future of freedom in America. Hub paused and listened, his sense of national identity—his patriotism—stirred. However much one might rail about the growing wealth gap in the U.S., and no matter how offensive one might find the treatment of the poor, of minorities, of those who hadn't boarded the platinum escalator of the information revolution, one thing remained true about the country, and that was the freedom its citizens enjoyed. Hub visualized the marble statue of Lincoln sitting in the memorial in Washington. Freedom. A word. A way of life.

A way of life in jeopardy. The crowd across the plaza cheered the speaker. A spontaneous chant ignited: "No fear! *No fear!*"

Hub turned and climbed the steps of the Federal Courthouse. His business there related to the outrage in full cry before Borough Hall, but was more specific, and enormously more practical, even though it involved obtaining a rather simple document. Within a minute he was ushered into the chambers of Judge Abraham Frankel.

A distant roar echoed through the windows: "NO FEAR! NO FEAR!"

The judge looked up from his desk. "Yes?" he said.

Hub said, "I want to talk about a free society."

At the CIA safe-house apartment, time ticked by. Sharon felt restless. Although Samir had promised to reveal more particulars about the meeting, he was remaining evasive. Earlier his vagueness had been understandable. Samir didn't like to disclose critical details until he felt confident he could deliver. But his confidence had been swelling ever since he'd seen the protest marchers on the TV. A new Samir seemed to have stepped forth, sure things would go well. Despite that, he still wasn't talking.

He pulled an expensive pocketknife from his pocket, then opened it and raised his arm. With unflinching strokes he sliced the stitches securing the transmitter.

Sharon drew her gun. "What are you doing?" she demanded.

Samir glanced indifferently at the gun. "West Bank rules, Sharon," he said, his tone almost bored. "You know you can't bring a gun." He walked past her to a closet. For a moment he assessed the contents, then started pulling out clothes. "Change of plans, woman," he declared, something in his voice quite different from before. "Do you want to meet them or not?"

Sharon stared at him. Samir's new attitude held a range of conceivable possibilities. Some could work out nicely. Others would spell disaster.

In the surveillance van, Colonel Hardwick cracked his knuckles. The microwave system was delivering pay dirt, quite possibly the key to liquidating the city's reign of terror. He reached for a handset radio, and said, "They're getting ready to move."

Samir tossed a robelike garment to Sharon. "A dress code," he explained. "They insist."

Sharon snarled, "If you're fucking with me . . ."

Samir yelled, "You want to meet them *or not*?" He sighed, his manner openly disparaging. "You must have faith, Sharon," he chided.

She studied him, her heart stilled. Years of experience with Samir had convinced Sharon that she knew him down to his Muslim soul. She wondered how much she'd missed. She had missed something. Deep things, she suspected, things that Samir hadn't revealed during the smoky late-night disquisitions on his brother the movie-lover, the seventy virgins waiting in paradise.

It stung her, the idea that the man she'd often thought a weakling could now, of all times, reveal unexpected dimensions. She examined the robe Samir had thrown. "Dress code," she muttered, crossing to a mirror. In it she inspected her hair, the minimal makeup she had on. She turned her head to check the look of her small pearl earrings.

Samir said acerbically, "We don't have much time."

"Units One and Two," Hardwick said into the handset radio. "On my signal . . ."

Tires squealed in the street outside the van. Something nudged it. The corporal checked a security monitor that provided an exterior view. Three late-model sedans, biggish, the kind the FBI used, had boxed in the van.

Hardwick exclaimed, *"What the . . . ?"*

Men were rousting Hardwick's people outside, busting the entire sound garden, seizing equipment. An agent spread-eagled a flabbergasted intelligence officer against a wall. With a deep Southern drawl, he said, "Hi, there, I'm new in town. Can you direct me to Carnegie Hall, or should I just go *fuck myself*?"

Danny Sussman appeared with a squad of NYPD detectives carrying confiscated electronics. Other agents used shotguns to blow off the surveillance van's rear doors. Hub clambered in. He checked out the glowing, blinking array of high-tech snoop equipment. To the incredulous Hardwick, he said, "Aren't you worried about exposure to all those microwaves and shit?" He started ripping out plugs at random. Screens went blank.

Minutes later Hub and Frank stood outside the safe-house apartment building. Hub rechecked the oscilloscope. Samir's green dot registered as a blinking light, indicating he should still be in the apartment. Which, if things were going according to plan, meant that Sharon hadn't moved as well.

"You gonna leave them up there?" Frank asked.

"Until they make contact," Hub replied.

"Nobody's come in or out for a while," Frank said. "They could both be dead up there."

Hub suddenly regretted that he'd disabled Hardwick's screens. They could have told him, probably down to heartbeats, the circumstances in the apartment. But it was too late to second-guess that decision; the NYPD had already towed the van away. He jerked his head at the building, wordlessly agreeing with Frank that too much time had gone by, and headed for the entrance. Frank followed.

In the hallway outside the apartment they paused to listen. Nothing but TV sound came through the door. Hub prepared to kick it in. Frank, worried now, said a silent prayer.

They burst through low and fast. An empty room greeted them. Just some blood on the floor, a small puddle. The transmitter, glistening, sat in it.

Frank keyed his radio. "Seal the building," he ordered.

Downstairs, backup agents burst into the lobby. They paid no attention to two women, with veiled faces and wearing traditional Arab *chadors*, walking away down the sidewalk.

"There better be a point to this," Sharon told Samir through her veil.

Samir smiled under his veil, relieved that the disguise ploy had worked. "Do not worry," he said.

They hurried off and melted into shadows.

Before Borough Hall the crowd continued to roar, "No fear! No fear!"

General Devereaux climbed out of his command Jeep a short distance away. The crowd's size and mood made him uneasy. Hardwick had alerted him to the possibility that the final terror cell was preparing to hit the march. But for reasons unclear to the general, Hardwick and his team had disappeared.

What bothered Devereaux most, however, stemmed from the protest itself. It was flouting his authority, the measures he had taken, the very legitimacy of martial law. Devereaux couldn't tolerate that. He needed a cowed populace if his strategy was to work. How could he flush out terrorists with thousands of people rampaging in the streets?

The situation required decisive remedies. Devereaux hadn't hesitated to order them. Soon he would have things back under control.

He checked his watch. Exactly on schedule, dozens of armored personnel carriers roared into Cadman Plaza. Soldiers in full riot gear poured from them. They formed battle lines along the perimeters, sealing off the plaza.

Devereaux watched a lieutenant raise a bullhorn. "This is an unlawful gathering," he proclaimed to the crowd. "You must disperse! I repeat, you must disperse!"

For a moment the crowd fell silent, aghast at the military force suddenly arrayed against them. The older among them recalled having seen similar sights in years past: Selma, 1963. Chicago, 1968. And South Central LA, 1993. Blood had been shed during each of those rents in the national fabric. Hatreds had boiled over, bringing turmoil and destruction to entire communities.

The protest speaker shook his head. He knew that only one response could save the day: solidarity. The simple but ultimately unstoppable force of People Power. "Join together!" he cried. "Join hands!"

Movement swirled through the thousands gathered as they linked arms. It made an improbable sight: Arab clerics joined with Hasidic rabbis, African-American civic leaders joined with Hispanic gang members. Their united front emboldened them. Louder than ever, they chanted, "No fear!"

The young soldiers in the battle line shot nervous looks at each other. How the hell could they use weapons against an "enemy" like this?

The crowd moved forward, directly at the massed soldiers.

Again the lieutenant raised his bullhorn. "These soldiers carry live ammunition," he announced as sternly as he could. "This is your final warning!"

Devereaux, watching, felt a surge of dread. The marchers advanced on his troops, closer and closer. Nothing in the general's lifetime of army service had prepared him for what he was seeing. Had he pursued his career with vigor and brains only to witness this?

At the crowd's forward edge a young girl unselfconsciously approached a soldier. She looked in his wide eyes and smiled. And then she simply walked past his gun.

More marchers passed by. The soldiers did nothing to stop them. In moments, the entire mass of the protesters was surging through the battle line.

Devereaux watched the engulfment of his men. He realized something about the American soul that he had long ago known, and revered. But had completely forgotten.

"No fear!" rang in the distance as Samir led Sharon down a street to a padlocked door. He produced a key from the folds of his robe and opened it. They went through into the entrance gallery of a *hammam*, an Arab bathhouse.

Steps descended to a misty tableau. Walls and arches were inlaid with mosaic tiles. Sunlight streamed from ornamental windows in the ceiling, playing on the steamy water of a sizable pool.

Samir closed the door and secured it. Sharon glanced around. No one else was there.

Hub and Frank moved through the protest marchers, scanning the crowd. Frank said angrily, "Either she's fucked us and gone over to the other side, or she's completely out of her head."

"It's what she's always wanted, Frank," Hub replied. "Think about it. She's been flying solo the whole time." He felt sick to his stomach. Sharon had betrayed him. He should have known she would do that—how could he have been so naive? And how could he justify busting up Hardwick's operation? The move now seemed a tremendous blunder.

Samir knelt at the pool's edge. He reached out to touch rising steam, then dipped his hand in the water, feeling its mineral-laden warmth.

"How soon are they coming?" Sharon demanded.

"They'll be here," Samir said serenely. He stood and started removing his clothes.

Sharon didn't like the look of that. Samir scarcely would decide to bathe if expecting a meet with a terror cell. "What are you doing?" she asked nervously.

The last garment came off. Naked, Samir stepped into the pool. He picked up a sponge. With ritual care, he started washing his body. "What message do you have for them, Sharon?" he inquired, his handsome face solicitous.

Sharon snapped, "I'll tell them when they're here." A bathhouse had figured in Samir's descriptions of the meet from the beginning. Panic corroded her mind as Sharon began to understand why.

Roaring voices trickled in through the skylights and echoed off the water, off the tiled walls: "No fear!" The march would pass the bathhouse, Sharon realized. In minutes the vanguard would be right outside.

Samir finished with his self-purification. He stepped from the pool and removed a towel from a hamper.

Sharon said, "There's nobody else coming, is there?"

"That's right," Samir said softly. He reached back in the hamper and brought out a Sig-Sauer 9mm automatic pistol.

"You're the last cell," Sharon said. Her hollow voice played across the pool.

"There will *never* be a last cell," Samir declared. He racked the Sig-Sauer's slide. "You should listen to the young men in the stadium. It is just the beginning."

He reached back into the hamper. With chilled fascination, Sharon watched a white robe billow out. Pure Egyptian cotton. A shroud. A funeral shroud.

Samir slipped it over his head.

Sharon blinked back tears of rage, of humiliation. Her man, her asset, had incontrovertibly revealed himself to be the last cell. The shroud said it all. Samir was the real deal.

She brought a hand to her ear. Samir didn't see her squeeze the earring on it.

28

Hub and Frank continued the search, the marchers only a block away and steadily advancing. The protest had taken on a triumphant air. As they flexed their civic might, citizens were discovering that outrage mixed well with exhilaration.

Frank didn't share that mood. He said disgustedly, "I've put out an alert at all three airports. *Kusacchtak!* She's gone. She could be halfway to . . ."

Something buzzed in Hub's pocket. The oscilloscope, he realized. He pulled it out. The green dot was blinking again. Weakly. Still, the signal had come back. Hub and Frank exchanged electrified glances.

Samir stood by the edge of the pool, his reflection playing in it, purifying in it, as he pulled street clothes over the shroud. The Sig-Sauer, shifting from hand to hand as he dressed, never strayed far from Sharon.

She said wanly, "How could I have missed the play?"

Samir replied with unexpected generosity. "It was the money," he said gently, going to the heart of their relationship, pointing out what had blinded her. "You believe money is power. Belief is power."

As if verifying that sentiment, the marchers' chant echoed louder through the skylights: "No fear!"

They were coming closer. *Lambs to the slaughter*, Sharon thought, having no one to blame now but herself. She couldn't hide her desperation. She exclaimed, "Just tell me we didn't finance your operation!"

Samir smiled sadly. "The world is a wheel," he remarked, his obliquity both softer and more crushing than a direct reply would have been. He sighed. "So"—his eyebrows rose—"what message do you have for me, Sharon?"

Sharon stared at the final cell, its membership of one. "They're going to release him," she muttered.

"Praise God," Samir murmured. "When will he be free?"

"A few months at most," Sharon replied quickly, hoping this would make a difference. "First, they have to bring him to trial, but—"

Samir turned to the hamper again, dismissing the importance of Sharon's disclosure. "No," he said flatly.

"But—" she sputtered. "That's what you want, isn't it? Why you've done all this?"

"No," Samir repeated. "It's not." From the hamper he drew a belt of Semtex plastic explosives. Velcro straps dangled from it; he used them to harness the belt around his chest. Then he approached Sharon, and said, "I want you to bleed. As we have bled."

"*Samir*," Sharon protested. "The Koran preaches . . ."

"Do not speak to me of the Koran, woman," Samir said in a rush, a tremor in his voice revealing the depths of his feelings, revealing the turmoil, hidden until now from Sharon, that had driven him to the decision to die. "You take our leader. A holy man. You put him in prison for preaching the word of God. You must learn the consequences of trying to tell the world how to live."

"But it's over," Sharon blurted. "Your point's been made, why spill any more blood?" Terror radiated from her eyes. "Those poor people out there in the street, they're fucking marching for *your* cause."

"Yes," Samir agreed, fastening the harness's last strap. He carefully drew out a knotted cord. The ripcord trigger, Sharon saw. "And they, too, will become its martyrs."

A voice boomed from the entrance gallery at the top of the stairs: "Let her go, you'll live!"

Sharon and Samir whirled to face the stairs. Hub stood atop them, aiming his .45.

Sharon blocked his shot at Samir.

Chants of "No fear!" poured through the partly open front door. The march's forward contingents had come much closer to the bathhouse.

Samir said in a low voice, "Move away from the door."

"*No!*" Sharon shouted.

Hub didn't move. His gun steadily aimed, he repeated, "Let her go, and you'll live."

"*Don't!*" Sharon howled.

Samir lost his cool. With sudden panic, he screamed, "*GET AWAY FROM THE DOOR!*"

Hub bellowed, "*Samir!*"

Samir screamed, "*YOU WANT TO DIE?*"

The voices reverberated through the misty air in colliding echoes, acoustically at war. Samir edged forward toward the stairs, forcing Sharon to precede him. And shield him.

But Hub continued to block the exit. "No way you're going out there," he said with tight calm.

Samir jammed his gun into Sharon's ribs. "Move away!" he shouted.

Hub locked eyes with Sharon. "Shoot," she said.

"Shut up," Hub said.

"Shoot," she said more loudly.

"*Shut up!*" Hub roared.

Samir pushed Sharon to the steps, then made

her mount them. Slowly they ascended. Sharon's eyes dueled with Hub's, exhorting him to do the thing that not only would finish the terror gripping the city, but end her own perdition—the hell of knowing that she had bankrolled every last cell. "*SHOOT ME!*" she screamed.

"I can't!" Hub shouted.

"You *have to!*" she begged, weeping now. Beseechingly, she said, "You"—tears streamed from her eyes—"*promised.*"

Her gaze gripped Hub with an almost physical force; as if subject to her will, his finger tightened on the trigger. But, almost imperceptibly at first, his aim wavered. Slowly the gun lowered.

"*No!*" Sharon yelled. She was sobbing.

Samir stared at the apparent surrender, his panic giving way to satisfaction. "It is God's will," he said. His left hand inched toward the ripcord.

Hub couldn't ignore a monstrous fact. The amount of Semtex strapped to Samir's chest would hurl a lethal curtain of projectiles directly at marchers passing the bathhouse. He said somberly, "If there is a God, He weeps at the crimes we commit in his name." Then he aimed and fired.

His first shot ripped through Sharon into Samir, blowing them both backward down the steps; the report thundered throughout the bathhouse. His second shot hit Samir's hand as it groped for the ripcord, smacking flesh to bits, blowing the hand away.

His third shot delivered the killing bullet directly to Samir's head. The impact rolled him into the pool.

A cloud of blood bloomed in the misty waters. The shroud billowed pinkly, a sunset cloud.

Hub knelt beside Sharon, the gunfire echoing off the tiles less and less loudly, a ricochet of fading ghosts. He pulled his radio and keyed it. "Officer down," he reported. "Officer down!"

Sharon's head lolled. She croaked, "Is he . . . Is he dead?"

"Shhhhhh . . ." Hub whispered, a hand pressing her shoulder. Blood gushed from her blouse.

Her eyes bleakly aglow, Sharon whispered, "No regrets . . ."

Hub leaned closer. One of her earrings caught his attention. It had been bent; Hub realized it contained the transmitter that had brought him here. "You knew," he whispered.

Sharon smiled with terminal sadness. "I . . ." she said softly, ". . . wondered."

Frank burst in; he surveyed the scene from the top of the stairs. Two paramedics rushed by him and down to Sharon. They pushed Hub aside to get at her, then launched into procedures to try to stabilize the trauma.

But Sharon was convulsing. Red spittle coursed from her mouth. "Sharon," Hub called. "*Sharon*," he exclaimed louder, hoping her name might sustain her.

"Emma," Sharon whispered. "My name is . . . Emma."

My God, thought Hub, newly aware of this woman's unending eerieness. She started mumbling. Hub listened to the incoherent voice, unable to make sense of what she was saying. Her voice clarified; Hub realized with a jolt that she was speaking in Arabic. "What?" he whispered. "What are you? I don't . . ."

The medics saw the futility of their mission. They drew back to give Hub room. Frank approached and stood over Hub. He listened to Sharon, then leaned closer, tears in his eyes. "'I seek refuge,'" he translated, his voice vibrating. "'King of kings . . .'"

It dawned on Hub that Elise, Sharon, Emma, this chimera of multiple identities, perhaps a riddle even to herself, was preparing to enter the next world without knowing what it held in store. He felt a rush of sorrow, so intense it banished everything else from his mind. Doomed already by her past, she had asked for death, begged for it, and now really was dying, with the knowledge that her passing wasn't wholly in vain—with the knowledge that sacrificing herself to stop Samir might have brought her a measure of redemption. Hub held her tenderly. She continued to murmur, praying to God, her Muslim God, in a mixture of two native tongues. Her voice grew weaker. "*Allah*

Akbar," she whispered. *"God is great . . ."*

"Allah Akbar," Frank echoed solemnly.

"Amen," Hub intoned.

Sharon's eyes glinted. For an instant they focused on Hub, transmitting a farewell salute. And then she was gone.

Hub stood. Samir floated in the pool, reddening the agency of his purification. Frank stared at Sharon, stunned by the knowledge of the common ground that he and she had shared when she lived, revealed only now with her death. The medics stood awkwardly at a distance, their radios squelching.

In the distance, chants of "No fear!" receded. The march had passed by. It was moving on.

29

Hub drove to the football stadium to finish a last piece of business. The accordion file that Chief of Staff Todd Franklin had given him rested on the rear seat.

At the perimeter fence he told the guards that he needed to see General Devereaux. He was waved through; staff people directed him to the locker-room command post. Hub entered it and closed the door behind him.

The general was watching TV news. "A very moving moment," the anchor said, "in which the people of a city step forward to declare their courage and solidarity."

Devereaux looked up, saw Hub, and said harshly, "Agent Hubbard, do you want to tell me exactly what you mean detaining Colonel Hardwick and six of my CID staff? Because that strikes me as a very peculiar idea of interagency liaison."

"It's over," Hub said simply, not reciprocating the general's angry tone.

"What's over?" Devereaux snapped.

"Samir was the last cell," Hub replied. "I took him down."

The general leaned back in his chair. "What makes you so sure he was the last cell?" he asked.

"Sharon," Hub replied.

"Sharon," Devereaux growled, "is not trustworthy."

"Sharon is dead," Hub declared, looking away. "Gave her life." He met the general's surprised stare. "They're going to release him," he said.

Devereaux's puzzlement deepened. "Release him?" he asked.

Hub held up the file. Casually, as if reciting the rap sheet of a street criminal, he said, "Clear violation of international law, United States statutory law, a couple of treaties, the federal perjury statute, and my favorite, the Logan Act, for conducting your own personal foreign policy."

Comprehension kindled in Devereaux's eyes.

"I know the whole story, General," Hub added without fanfare.

"You don't know shit," Devereaux said sourly. "Poor suffering Sharon and her poor suffering people. It's called 'going native'—the most elementary error of an intelligence operative, and she made it. She had all of you working for her, and she was working for *them* without even knowing it. And now they're getting exactly what they want, which is the sheik is back in the mix. But ten times as strong, because now he's the big man who stood up to the Americans." He gave Hub a contemptuous glance. "I did what was necessary. I make no apologies. If you think you're going to be able to use that file against me, you know even less about politics than I imagined."

"General," Hub said patiently, "I'm not *in* politics. You can have this back. I won't use it." Hub handed Devereaux the file.

Devereaux took it, his jaw muscles working. "Don't expect me to get all weepy with gratitude," he remarked. "You serve your country." He glanced at his watch. "Is there anything else?" he asked, his voice dismissive.

Hub gazed at the pugnacious face, itching to haul back and clock it. The general took note of Hub's feelings; his eyes twinkled, signaling amusement. Hub exhaled. Then he extracted a document from his jacket's inside pocket. "This is a writ of *habeus corpus* from the U.S. District Court," he explained. "Demanding the release all those being held here without legally valid cause." He cocked his head inquiringly. "Are they free to go?"

Devereaux considered the question. "No," he said.

They stared at each other, seemingly in a standoff that didn't favor Hub. Devereaux smiled. He said, "You might just be old enough to remember . . . 1957. Governor Orval Faubus defied the Supreme Court and refused to desegregate the schools in Little Rock, Arkansas. Who'd they call, son, to defend civil rights, when those laws you just memorized weren't even on the books?"

Yeah, right, Hub thought. *The laws I just memorized.*

"Did they call their congressman?" Devereaux continued. "Did they call the FBI? Who'd they call to walk six-year-old black kids home from school?" He tapped the Airborne patch on his shoulder. "They called us." He glanced coolly at Hub. A patriarch dispensing wisdom to a hothead who someday would understand, he said conclusively, "It's *never* simple."

Well, thought Hub, looking Devereaux straight in the eye, *sometimes it is simple.* "William Devereaux," he said, his tone now not casual at all, "you are under arrest for the torture and murder of Tariq Husseini under color of authority, United States Code Title 42, Chapter 21, Subchapter 1, Sections 1983." He drew his gun. "It's very simple," he informed the general. "Surrender your weapon."

Devereaux's jaw dropped.

Behind Hub the door flew open. Shouts eddied in amid sounds of commotion. The cause became evident when Frank and several other agents forced their way past bewildered military staff. A swarm of reporters followed. Armed with still cameras, videocams, and glaring TV lights, they shouted questions.

Hub confiscated the stunned general's gun. He read him his rights, then cuffed him. Strobes flashed. Cams rolled tape. The reporters shouted more questions, their hostility and pointedness making it clear that the general would face more shouts, lots of them, for a long time to come.

Half an hour later outside the stadium, a cop car pulled away with its blue lights flashing. Devereaux sat in the rear seat.

Hub stood with Frank near the tunnel that led to the arena. Women and small children stood vigil outside the perimeter security fence, as they had since the detention of their husbands, fathers, and sons. Hub and Frank wanted to see their reaction to something they were not expecting.

The tunnel's barricades opened. Hundreds of boys and young men surged forth, shouting with amazement and happiness. Surprised relatives called to them. Boys ran to the opened arms of their mothers, men to the tearful smiles of their wives and children. Hub watched the reunions, grateful finally to witness something uplifting. Positives had been scarce for far too long.

Frank shook his head. In a tone that mingled relief with frustration he asked, "Did we win or did we lose?"

Hub had no answer. No one had an answer to that question.